THE MACKON COUNTRY

THE MACKON COUNTRY

MARTIN KEAVENEY

PENNILESS PRESS PUBLICATIONS

www.pennilesspress.co.uk/books

Published by

Penniless Press Publications 2021

ISBN 978-1-913144-32-6

Cover Image: Drying Turf – Paul Butler

For Bernie

Through the Perspex I saw Ash. He lay on the edge of the road behind the jeep. The red ball he'd been chasing had rolled across to the hawthorn ditch. His head lifted a little, the eyes darted, the body couldn't match the movement, the breath was tiny puffs in the air. It took me a couple of seconds to react, like I was on pause, a framed still in a nightmare. I turned, knocking over the neat green pile of my new first year copybooks. 'Dad! Ash has been hit!'

The image of the laptop screen was reflected in the window behind the far sofa bed. Human-like creatures walked along a dusty road amongst crumbled buildings and abandoned cars. They were like suspended puppets, with sections of stomachs, limbs missing, yet they kept walking. Dad paused the stream and looked up.

Outside, the evening was cool, summer fading, it was darkening at half eight. There was a short patch of ground between the mobile home and the road. I ran across in my bare feet, green and yellow weeds spiking my heels, dad following. The jeep engine had died, the driver's door opened, sand-boots pressed into the ground. Midnight stepped out. He puffed on a King Edward.

'I'm after hitting a dog,' Midnight said to the phone at his ear. He reached into the jeep and pulled out a six-pack of Dutch Gold. 'No, a dog…I'll see you at half three so, Paddy.' He put the phone into his jacket pocket and looked at me. 'He came out of nowhere. I nearly went into the ditch.'

'He was after the poxy ball,' dad said, as he came close. 'He's blind in one eye. Shouldn't be on the phone anyway, should you, Midnight?' Ash had been half-blind when we got him, born like that, the people at the pound reckoned. We'd got him a few weeks after mam went away. He was a kind of replacement, there was definitely more life in the dog. Dad looked up through The Mackon village street and then left, out the road to the bog. 'We better get him in.'

Ash's head was still now, the eyelids blinked, he stared down the field, to the collapsed cottage at the end, hidden with ivy.

'Should you move him before the vet gets here though?' I said. Dad stared at me.

'I've no credit. I don't suppose you have, Tommy. Midnight?' Midnight handed dad his phone.

'Go easy. Not much on her either, Joe.'

Dad took the phone and rubbed his thumb on the screen. 'Sixty for a call out. You'll cover that will ya, Mid?'

'Fuck it, I got hammered this evening. Canter at Newhaven. Fixed, it had to be.'

'I thought that was how your system worked?' Dad stood back from my uncle. 'Jesus, smell of porter! Where were ya?'

'Down in The Tree. I only had a few. Waiting for Pock to ring. I didn't want to be talking about it at home with her there. She came early on, going on about a turkey dinner.'

'Ah, the loins, the loins…how are you cleaned out again already, it was only the twenty-fifth last week?'

'Pock and the young lad just got the yoke on a truck,' Midnight said. 'Young lad got a van as well, but he was mad—'

'Will you keep your voice down! I told ya, I don't want to hear about it! I don't trust that bastard.'

A white Ford Fiesta van, 1992, passed by at twenty miles an hour, the driver's window down, local radio blaring. Tuohy sucked on a lollipop, stared at Ash as he drove. The van turned right at the boreen just at the end of The Mackon village street.

'Prick. You'd think he'd keep his eyes on the road,' Dad said.

'He knows the way home so well, he could do it blindfold,' Midnight said.

'More cheapo stakes in the back, did ya clock that? He has us tormented with his cattle breaking in—'

'Joe, why don't you do this job instead of that young fella. I'm going up at one tonight. Pock won't care—'

'Will you shut your mouth, alright?'

'Dad, the vet?' Dad looked at Ash, the black fur with specks of grey getting matted now with blood. He took a deep breath, then handed the phone back to Midnight. I was confused. 'Dad! He could be running out of time! What's going on? What about the vet?'

'I think it's a bit late for the vet now, son.'

'But he's still alive, he's breathing?' Dad knelt, gathering Ash up. The dog whined. 'Are you sure you can move him like that?'

'We need to get him off the road.'

'Are you bringing him inside, dad?' Dad walked toward the mobile. There was a large blood stain left on the road.

'Come on son.' Midnight took my shoulder. Dad had turned and gone around the side of the mobile with Ash. I ran toward him, catching my breath.

'Dad? Where are you bringing him?' Dad had lain the dog on the ground in front of what was to have been our sitting room window, but for some years now had remained just a windowsill. There were two lines of blocks either side through which Tuohy's wandering cattle sometimes looked out, plastic damp course flapped at the edges, moss and green water stains coated the walls. I stopped at the gas cylinder. 'Dad? The vet? Come on!' Midnight was at the corner, running his cigar hand through grey curls. The ground was soft here, opened for the new house, it was less settled then the field beyond. I realised then it was the easiest place for digging. 'Dad? What are you doing?'

Dad stood back from Ash, leant against the windowsill. He pulled out a squashed box of Major, lit up, instantly the stink of nicotine hit the air. 'It's a bit of a problem, Tommy.'

'What problem?'

'Sixty euro for a call out. That problem. The vet won't even look at Ash for less.'

4

'You could pay him later. He wouldn't just let him die. He's a vet, they care more about animals than money. Midnight, what about Ann, can you ring her, maybe she'd help us?'

'Hmm. She's not too happy with me at the moment, I'd say. I was meant to be back for that dinner a long time ago.' Midnight scratched his jaw.

'He's only goin' to put him down anyway, Tommy. We don't have poxy pet insurance for painkillers, leg ops and all that jazz. Do you know the cost of morphine and anti-whatever they're called?'

'Dad, you don't know what he'll do. You want to just leave him there to die, is that it?'

'No son, I'm won't do that...'. As he spoke, I saw what was going to happen. I ran around the mobile, past Midnight. 'Tommy!'

Inside, I pulled at the press door over the cooker. I looked on the counter, the table, around dad's double bed. The keyring rattled as he came in.

'No dad, please!' I stood between him and the press.

'Settle down son. The dog is in pain out there.' Always willing to please, Ash whined into the night.

'You can't do this, it's inhumane!'

'Come out of my way!'

'No!'

Dad took me by the shoulder, fingers gripping my bones, pushed me with power onto the near sofa bed, my leg rammed the corner of the table, pain spread. Dad slickly slid in the small key, the door clicked open. He pulled out the parts: barrel, block, butt, levers, springs, the magazine.

'No dad, please.' I was shaking now, standing at the table.

'I need to get this done, isn't the animal in pain!' He already had the rifle assembled.

I stood at the door. I could smell his meaty breath, the thick underarm sweat, the faint hint of piss where he'd dribbled. He slid a round into the mag. and clicked it on the underside of the barrel.

'It's time.' He drew back the bolt.

'No, daddy!' Dad towered over me, a foot and a half at least, hair knotted over his thick arms, the shirt partly buttoned, grey chest curls spilling out, his head shining in the yellow ceiling.

'Come out of my way!' He was sick of this, I could tell.

'Please!' It had started raining, a fine drizzle you could hardly see, but I could hear the tiny pin pricks landing on the roof. It always made me feel safe in the middle of the night. Dad pushed past me. As he went outside, dark stains grew on his white t-shirt. When I followed him, the large blob of my uncle got in the way.

'Come back in, Tommy,' Midnight said. Dad disappeared with the rifle around the back.

'No!' I shouted after him.

'There's nothing you can do.'

'Let me see him before…'. My vision was glassy. It was really going to happen, dad was going to shoot my dog. I couldn't get any more words out. I pushed forward, but Midnight's grip tightened, he was too strong. 'It's easier this way, lad.'

My nose was blocked, my eyes stung as Midnight pulled me back in. Inside, I could still hear dad moving around the back. Midnight sat across from me, opened a can. Through the Perspex, I could see the outline of dad standing over Ash in the dusk. The thin end of the weapon was pointed at my dog's head.

'Now, don't be looking at that.' Midnight pulled the smoke-blackened blind down, he took out the yellow cigar box and unwrapped another smoke. He found his Zippo in a jeans pocket. As he sparked up an orange flame, the shot rang out.

I lay down, turned to the pillow, wishing I was somewhere else, unable to kill off the image of the bronze hollow point round smashing through Ash's skull.

'We'll get you another one, lad,' Midnight said, as he took his can up. 'It's a short life for a dog, and yer man was getting on anyway.'

Now I heard the spade being picked up off the concrete subfloor in the new house where dad had flung it in a temper weeks ago. The digging began, sharp slices in the earth, levering up the clay. The rain had gotten heavier, the pin pricks on the roof had become a blanket of dull drilling. I could hear the jerking out of loose stones, heaving of the dirt as it was tossed in a pile. 'Maybe you want a cup of tea?' I heard Midnight fill the saucepan, light the gas. 'Where are all the cups?' I turned around, saw him root through the press. He definitely wasn't going to wash any of the mugs piled high in the sink. Eventually he came over with a steaming beaker, the lid of my Roughneck flask from sixth class. When he put the tea beside me, he looked

7

at the folded clothes at the end of the bed, light blue shirt and navy jumper, grey trousers. 'Starting school?'

'Tomorrow.' He looked at the crest. 'You're going to Ballincalty Secondary? Why didn't he send you to Cloonloch?'

'I'd have needed a bus ticket.'

'If he was organised he could have got one. Ballincalty is a bit…'.

'Rough. I heard.'

'Go in by the football pitch in the morning. That's what we used to do to keep out of the Wet Room.'

'The what?' The noise out the back had changed, fresh clay being returned to the hole, over Ash's remains, back in the same place, but not in the same way.

'That'll take your mind off the little dog.'

'What will? The "Wet House"?'

'"Wet Room". No, no, going to school. Sure, it doesn't matter which one it is anyway, you'll do well. All these books you have. You did good in the village school. You take after your mother. She had brains that one. See all them?' He nodded at a pile of volumes on anatomy under dad's bed. 'They were hers, when she went to college for a while that time.'

'Does she not still have them?'

'What?'

'Brains?'

'Oh, she does, she does. Not like me. I could barely spell me name at school. But Sheila was bright. I remember her packing up all them books for college. Getting the bus down the country. She loved it, she'd be on about lectures, debates and all that.'

'Why did she leave?'

'Ah, she lost her way. I was in there this evening. An awful sight—'

'Can you turn off the big light?'

I pulled the blanket over my head, Midnight slurped his can, dad raked the clay level, the rain still hitting the roof above. I woke once, I thought one of the other textbooks in the pyramids had slid off the table, but it might have been the gunshot going off again in my dreams.

I put some stones around Ash's grave. He was already breaking down underneath the scraws. I wondered had the earwigs and beetles got to him yet. I knelt and said a prayer. Images came of Ash running through the boggy acres of heather and marsh around The Mackon. I saw him race across the hawthorn ditches, finding a shady spot in the site on a summer's day, in the cool under the mobile during a downpour, or nosing through gaps in the stones underneath the ivy at the collapsed cottage.

I saw Ash eating dried pellets in the purple doggy bowl with white paws dad had lifted from Tesco one quiet Sunday. I saw him snoozing under the table as I tried to sleep, Midnight and dad playing cards until dawn, my uncle slurping cans of Dutch Gold and chewing King Edwards as he went on about his heroics out in 'The Leb', dad puffing Majors and sipping coke. Then I saw Ash trusting his one good eye as he tracked the red ball that cost him his life.

Some clay had gotten stuck on my school trousers. I tried to wipe it off. I'd woke early before seven. There were cans on the table, the ashtrays overflowed. Midnight's jeep was gone, and there was no sign of him or dad. I found sixty cents in change on the far sofa bed, slid the textbooks in my schoolbag, tidied my new light blue shirt.

At eight o'clock, it was time to start walking. I took one of dad's Cokes from the fridge and drank it as I left. I walked by the blood stain on the side of the road, the red ball was still in the ditch. I passed Tuohy's boreen. I could see his white Fiesta parked at the cottage. I went up through The Mackon village, by Sweeney's bar and shop on the left, the windows and doors boarded up with faded ply for as long as I could remember. Further on, dying summer weeds had grown in the playground at the back of our national school. Even Kilroy's garage looked abandoned, although I knew the mechanic would arrive soon in overalls. There were lines of stripped cars on the oil-stained gravel. At the front, dad's Avensis had been parked for months — it was still 'waiting for parts'. Only the church at the end, where the road turned for Ballincalty town, looked alive, with its mown grass, tarmac and rows of pine.

'Death Notices' played somewhere on local radio, a purple Micra came from Ballincalty. The car stopped beside me, the driver's window rolled down. 'Tommy!' Ann looked out at me, large ring earrings dangling. 'What are you doing out here? Your dad texted me. He and Jeremy got word of some security work late last night. I'm to bring you to school.' She smiled as I got in the passenger side. 'You have everything with you? First day, isn't it?'

Ann controlled the steering wheel by edging her thumbs around the base, her e-fag lit up as she dragged, little puffs of artificial smoke floated out. Rosary beads hung around the rear-view mirror, a statue of Our Lady was stuck to the dash. Some of the glue had spilt, ran down the

11

front, it had hardened into a permanent stain. Part of the figure had come loose, and Our Lady tapped her right foot as we drove along the bog road to town. 'I had a lovely bit of Goulash for Jeremy yesterday evening, but he never came home at all after he went to visit your poor mother. Not a call nor anything. What do you think of that carry-on, Tommy?'

It took about five minutes to get to Ballincalty. The terraced housing on the single street gave it the look of a town. We pulled in at O'Malley's service station, beside the gates to the school avenue. I filled a tenner unleaded into the Micra. In the shop, students of all shapes and sizes pushed around. They were all familiar with each other as far as I could see. The rest of sixth class from The Mackon village school had gotten the school bus to Cloonloch College, six miles further on. I knew no one. Most of the people who could afford it avoided Ballincalty Secondary. Down at the deli counter, a blonde lad in an apron arranged paninis, gourmet sandwiches, Cornish pasties under a glass display.

'Can I get a small sausage roll?' I said.

The lad looked at me. 'A mini roll? That's all? One mini roll?'

'Maurice! Maurice!' The youth looked across the shop to the tills. O'Malley himself glared back, purple-skinned, squeezed into a shirt. 'The scones! Get them out of the oven! Now!' Maurice tossed my sausage roll into a paper bag, slapped a sticker on it and left it on the glass. Someone bumped against me. I turned around. A boy of my height slipped a Kellogg's breakfast bar into his pocket as he turned the aisle.

At the counter, a queue had formed. O'Malley and two women wearing green shop jumpers took orders of breakfast rolls, biros, multicoloured foolscaps, chocolate biscuits, soft drinks. There was a girl with long blonde hair at the counter. She looked like a first year, she was buying chewing gum. O'Malley served her, smiling as he handed her the change. 'Have a great first day, Rebecca!'

The Kellogg's bar lad was next. I couldn't hear what he ordered. 'Johnny Marley's son?' O'Malley said. 'And does he know you're in here buying tobacco? What are you, twelve? I'll give you "Twenty B & H", go on, get out of my sight, or you'll have a taste of me boot!' O'Malley spoke himself into a roar, spit flying across the counter. Marley made a 'cool it' sign with his fingers as he left, O'Malley's head was shaking.

We drove up the avenue lined with poplars. At the top, on the left, there was a tall square building, roughcast with small windows and green battered doors. 'That used to be the convent, before Mr Sherlock and the school took over,' Ann said, as we rounded an island of more poplar trees and came into the front carpark, which was full of buses and wandering students. 'Have a good first day, Tommy. I hope your father is back this evening. You look very smart in your uniform. You have everything? Your lunch and that?' I nodded and got out.

I walked toward the entrance, through groups of teenagers, most of them taller than me, they shouted and laughed over my head. There was a large group of girls at the front of the bus by the entrance doors. They weren't moving, they just stood chatting and blocking the way. I went down the end of the bus to get past them. There was a shout behind me. Marley came running. Two tall boys followed, one was Maurice without his apron, but there was still deli flour on his hands. Marley went around the bus and dived behind a bush at the wall.

'Where'd he go?' Maurice said to me, at the corner of the bus. I looked down the side of the building.

'In there,' I pointed at a green door.

'Good man!' Maurice and the other lad ran toward the door, the bush moved a little.

'Hey Mo!' A voice came from the poplar island. Another tall student came out of the greenery, tossing a fag butt on the tarmac. He nodded at the bush. Maurice turned, reached in and grabbed Marley by the neck. An arm came around my head suddenly. 'Another smart cunt!'

Before I could even turn, we were inside the green door. It was a long musty hall, cracked vinyl tiles, high ceilings, peeling wallpaper, coving crumbling. I struggled but the grip was too tight.

'Let me go!' I heard Marley. There was laughter.

We came through another doorway into a courtyard-type space, surrounded with walls, doors, three stories above with balconies. There were rusting gates tossed on the ground, worn and upended cobbles, scattered scraps of wood, some stacked window frames.

'You can't do this anymore, it's illegal,' Marley said.

'Shut it!' A palm smacked off Marley's skull. We stopped at another doorway.

'You'll be locked up for this!'

'Like you should be, you little thief.' It was Maurice. 'You think I didn't see you all summer coming into our shop lifting things?'

'What are you on about? You've no proof!' Maurice pulled Marley straight up, pushed his hand into Marley's pocket, the Kellogg's bar slipped out. Maurice smiled.

'There's my proof. Do you think we are buying this stuff so you can come and take it for free? You little snake!' Maurice made a clearing throat sound, then spat a ball of phlegm, which landed across Marley's freckles. Someone clicked a phone cam.

'Let's get them inside.' They pulled us through a doorway. It was an ancient gents' toilet, a blackened channel ran along the wall. The washbasin had been ripped out, only rusting pipework remained. There was a dirty bowl in a cubicle to one side. Part of the door was still attached to the hinges.

'Welcome to the Wet Room, girls!' Maurice opened his fly, pulled his lad out and filled the toilet bowl.

'Are you sure about this, Maurice? His ol' man being a lawyer and all?'

'You wouldn't be stupid enough to tell daddy about this now, would you, Jacqueline? You know we have all your thefts on camera.'

Marley struggled. 'That's not legal proof.'

'Shut it!' Another smack across the skull.

'That was a bit dry in there, but it's ready now.' Maurice nodded happily, zipping himself up. 'Go on lads, stick his fucking head in it!'

'No!' Marley was squealing as they dragged him over the rim. I cringed as they pushed his head deep. They let him up after a couple of seconds, piss dripping from his jaw.

'Your ol' man might be able to pull a few strings for thieving scumbags like you in a court, but there's nothing he can do for you in Ballincalty Secondary,' Maurice said. 'Didn't think of that, did you, Jacqueline? Daddy should have sent you on the buseo to Cloonloch with all his money, but he was too tight.'

Tears rolled down Marley's face, mixing with the yellow beads on his cheeks and the remains of Maurice's phlegm on his nose, drops of the mixture clung to his hair. Someone took another picture. 'Remember Jacqueline, any word of this little party and this pic. goes public on Facebook!'

'You'll never get the ride in your life after!'

'I wouldn't say this fairy would be fit for that type of work anyway.'

'Let him go!' I said in a burst. Maurice looked at me.

'Don't worry, young lad, you'll get a go too. Bring him over here, lads.' They tossed Marley to the wall, one of them pinning him there with a boot firmly in the chest, while the others dragged me to the cubicle.

'Who is this?' Maurice said.

'What's your name, fag?' One of the others stared at me, his face almost touching mine.

'O'Toole.'

'Oh, I know this fella.' Another of the Leaving Certs nodded behind. 'He lives in a caravan out in the bog.

16

In The Mackon. The ghost village. The father is a pure sponger.'

'What are you living in a caravan for? Dad too fucking lazy to work?'

'Knack-a-lacks, are ye?'

'It's a mobile home, not a caravan.'

'Oh, a "mobile home", sorry. Something against the Travellers, have ya?'

'Racist type cunt, is he?'

'Wait'll the McDonaghs in fourth year hear about this.'

'They won't be too happy, Mo.'

'They will not. You think the Wet Room is bad?'

'It'll be a funfair compared to what they'll do to ya, scan.'

'Fuck this! Get him in the pot!' They pulled me over to the rim, pushed my head toward the white bubbles, the piss smell was so strong, I thought I'd puke. I closed my eyes.

'Hey!' It was a voice from the courtyard. 'That calf is from The Mackon. What did he do?'

'Covered for this snake lawyer's son. New first year.'

'Looks like he's had enough.'

Grips were released. I looked out the doorway to the light. I barely recognised Gerry Sweeney from the closed down shop in The Mackon. He'd been one of the 'big lads' in the village school when I was in Baby Room.

Me and Marley were tossed out a side door into a path near a football pitch. I took out my phone as Marley found an outside tap and washed his face. It was twenty past ten, we'd already missed three classes and we hadn't a clue where to go. We didn't even know how to get back inside the school. 'Dirty bastards,' Marley said, as he dried his face with his sleeve. 'They'll pay for that. They will pay.'

We followed the path along the old convent wall and came into a thick area of poplars, hawthorns, gorse and beech trees. Eventually we reached a wire fenced area, tennis courts with the nets all removed. Down steps beyond, there were double doors leading inside.

'What happened with Maurice?' I said, as we walked.

'Just because I took the odd bar. Mean bastards. O'Malley himself is in bankrupt shite. The ol' lad came across him a few times up in the High Court. It probably didn't help.'

We went through the double doors into a square area with a red floor, walled benches, doors to classrooms amongst the blockwork, the end of a stairs.

'Your ol' lad is a lawyer?'

'Solicitor. He has a practice in town.'

'Ye must be loaded so. What do you need to steal for?'

'I don't need to. Did ya never lift anything?'

'No. What—'

'What is going on here?' It was McDermott, the Vice-Principal. He stood at the foot of the stairs, holding a folder.

'We got lost, sir,' Marley said.

'Got lost? And where are your name badges?'

McDermott got our badges from the secretary's office and lectured us about the 'importance of organisation' as he led us to the French room. 'Sorry to interrupt, Mrs Petit,' the V.P. said, as he opened the door into a large classroom. The teacher turned around from the whiteboard. She'd just written 'Bonjour'. 'I found these boys wandering around the Resource Area. According to their timetable, they are part of this class.'

'Thank you, Vice-Principal.' The blonde girl from the shop, Rebecca, smiled in the front row. Me and Marley went down to the back of the room.

We followed the class around all morning until someone gave us a timetable. Most of the group seemed to know each other well, but the other Ballincalty kids didn't seem too fond of Marley. He sat beside me as we all had lunch in the Resource Area. I'd finished my cold sausage roll and was taking out my new books to have a look, when Marley pulled me by the arm. 'Come on for a fag, Tommy.'

'I don't smoke.'

'Come for the craic anyway.'

Marley led me out the double doors, up the steps through the tennis courts, where the Leaving Certs played soccer. Maurice sat watching in a corner, smoking a fag which was carefully hidden behind curled fingers. My phone rang as we got to the wood. The number was withheld.

'Hello?'

'Howya lad!'

'Hi dad.'

'Started school alright? Ann brought ya?'

'Yeah.'

'Fair play to her. We got a bit of security work. Up the country. Just got word late last night. You were fast asleep. There's a good few quid in the job. I'll be able to get the Avensis sorted out from the garage.'

'Oh. That's good.' Marley led me through the dirt path amongst the poplars. We passed groups of students hidden behind greenery, watching the double doors as they sucked on fags. 'Will you be back this evening, dad?'

'Don't know. It depends on what the boss man says, son. I'll get Ann to collect you if I have to.'

'Where are you working anyway?'

'I've to go, Tommy. Credit's out. Good luck.'

Marley had found a vacant gorse bush which had fairly good cover from the doors. He pushed into the middle of it, opened his fly and pulled out a box of Purple Silk Cut. 'I've only a few left. That ol' wank O'Malley stopped play this morning.' Marley handed me one. It felt strange in my hand. I'd watched dad smoke them for years. I'd always hated the smell of nicotine. I'd been proud of my clean lungs as dad coughed, Midnight choked on filthy cigars. I'll never smoke, I'd always said, yet here I was lighting one of the things. It tasted awful. I coughed out the smoke, it took a few pulls to get it to go down my throat. It was like I was trying to write with my weak hand. In my chest the smoke felt heavy.

'They're rotten,' I said.

'Don't worry,' Marley blew out a blue smoke ring. 'They get better quick.'

I saw a flash of blonde through the wire netting. Rebecca walked with two girls from our class, one with tight brown curly hair, the other wore huge heavy-rimmed glasses under an orange candyfloss cloud. Marley followed my gaze.

'Who do ya fancy? The blondie one, I suppose. Everyone's after her. Don't waste your time with that mug on ya. You should try them dogs with her, Karen and Suzanne. They're more in your line, scan.'

At four o'clock I stood at the entrance waiting for Ann or dad. I watched Marley run down the avenue, Maurice and others chasing him. My head still stung from the sharp slap the Deli King had served up on the way out. The Principal, Sherlock, came out of the Assembly Hall. He was shorter than the V.P., but with his bullet head and dark eyes, he looked fiercer. He glanced at the name badge the V.P. had given me.

'Ah, Mr O'Toole. What happened this morning?'

'Got lost, sir.'

'With Mr Marley?'

'Yes sir.'

'Are you waiting for someone?'

'I…yes.'

'Perhaps you need a lift? Out to The Mackon? My car is here.' Sherlock nodded at an 07 Avensis parked right at the door.

'No thanks, sir. I'd say my dad will be here soon.'

'Very well.' He turned inside and then looked back at me. 'Mr Marley is not the best guide around these parts. See to it you place yourself in alternative company.'

'Yes sir.'

Sherlock went off toward the Resource Area, oncoming students careful to keep the far side of the corridor. I watched the country kids pile onto buses, the last of the townies hurry out the avenue. Someone stopped behind me. It was Rebecca. As I turned around, she glanced up, her brown eyes on me. I froze for a second, I couldn't breathe.

'Find your way round yet, Tommy?'

I made myself smile. 'Ha-ha. Waiting for a lift?'

'Mum's late for everything. Probably the same here too.'

There was a pause. Even though I wanted to keep talking, I also wanted to escape, the tension was awful, what if I said something really stupid, would she tell all her friends? She scrolled on her phone.

'You on Facebook?' I said.

'Of course.' She looked up, like she was going to say something else. A 12 Audi swung around the poplar island, a blonde woman driving, wearing sunglasses. Rebecca slid away her phone, pulled her schoolbag up on her shoulder.

'See you tomorrow, Tommy.'

'See ya.' She was gone again. It was like someone had turned off all the lights in the world. Maybe I could message her later about homework, I thought then, as I saw Ann's Micra come through the avenue gates.

St. Michael's Nursing Home was on the outskirts of Cloonloch. It was a converted national school. The tall Georgian windows and high ceilings reminded me of The Mackon village school classrooms every time we went there. There was a long hall of curling lino with wards to one side.

Someone pulled my arm as we came into mam's unit. I could smell strong perfume. 'Gerald? Gerald?' Nora let go of my arm. The woman that slept in the first bed stared at me. 'I'm going home this evening. I thought you were my son.' She straightened her red dress and left down the handle of a green suitcase.

I leant against the radiator at the window by mam's bed. Ann put Lucozade on the bedside locker, sat on the visitor's chair. When I'd started going to St. Michael's first, it had seemed like a lunatic asylum, the figures grinning in the hall, twisting dishcloths in clawlike grips, others feeling their way by the radiator. The noise was the worst, yells every few minutes, the low hum of country and western music, rattling trolleys, slamming doors. There was a smell of floor cleaner everywhere. But mostly I didn't notice these things anymore, only the sudden beat of an industrial washing machine on spin cycle, or an aluminium plate cover crashing would break through. Everything else had melted into the background, like the paint and the tiles. Just like the residents often faded away, one week tugging at a blanket, fumbling with a beaker of cold tea and mashed up biscuit, the next nothing left there only a mattress, or no bed at all, locker, iron wardrobe swept away in a flash. When I was younger, dad said these vanishing patients had been moved to another ward, with a better view of the garden, or maybe they wanted to hear another radio station. There were only three residents in mam's ward, mam down the very end, Nora always standing by the door, waiting for Gerald to collect her, the third parked at the window across from us. She groaned every few minutes, staring at the ceiling, blanket tucked around her chin.

'So there's no news from The Mackon really,' Ann was saying. 'Joe and Jeremy are gone up the country doing a bit of work for a few days, some man they worked for before. I cooked a lovely Goulash for us on Sunday evening and Jeremy never came back at all.'

Mam sniffed in the seat at the window. She wore a white cardigan, grey skirt and slippers. Her hands were together on her lap, there was an ID band clipped to her wrist. 'Pat?' she said, her voice croaking.

'I don't know how he served in the army, he has no discipline.' Ann puffed on her e-fag. 'Doesn't Tommy look very handsome in his uniform?' Mam looked at her hands. 'I said I'd bring him in to see you, first day at the school and all.'

'Pat?' Mam said, looking to the hall, as though she'd seen something there.

Ann heated some beef casserole she'd made for me back at the mobile. I took out my homework diary, looked at my new timetable.

'Did you get much homework?' She brought the steaming bowl over to the table.

'No. First day.'

'When the lessons start, you want to keep on top of it, Tommy. Glass of milk?'

'Thanks. When's dad coming back?'

'Tomorrow, I think. Now, I need to go and get my own home in order. You'll be alright to wash up, won't you? If I don't hear from Joe, I'll be over at eight in the morning to bring you, okay?'

'Thanks, Ann.'

As Ann drove off, I tossed the plate in the sink. I took out my books. We hadn't done a lot at school, just looked through the courses really. The words were exciting: 'modules', 'syllabus', 'texts', even 'Christmas Exams'. The geography teacher had given us a short exercise. We had to write a paragraph on what we knew about the Earth's layers. I opened my copybook, wrote a sentence. I took out my phone, clicked on Facebook. A first-year group had been set up by the prefects. I'd gotten an invitation. I accepted and quickly found Rebecca. I clicked on her page. There was a great photo of her. DOB – 9 June 1999. Music – Taylor Swift, Adele. Favourite place – France. There were just a couple of other photos, one with her mother, them sitting on two deckchairs, a tray of drinks between them at a beach. Rebecca had only joined up a few months earlier, her timeline gave little more away. I clicked on the message icon. The cursor blinked. 'How are you?' seemed way too boggy, too The Mackon. 'Doing your homework?' was old-fashioned. 'Hey' probably too friendly. I tried out a few versions. My finger slid on the screen too quick and I sent her a message by accident. It read 'Sxxx'.

I woke to groaning cattle. One of their huge heads banged against the Perspex, breath blowing up steam clouds. I pulled on my trousers and shoes, ran out. I shooed the cattle through the site, down the field, one ran in the doorway. There was a splash as his hole spat out a thick wave of green shite all over the floor of what was to have been our sitting room. I got them down to the end, some tried to get around the ivy, into the cottage ruin, but I turned them back through the gap they had tramped. Two of Tuohy's cheapo stakes were on the ground. I pulled up one of the strands of tangled barbed wire, hooked it on a branch as a temporary block and hurried across Tuohy's fields to his cottage. It was no wonder the cattle wanted to feast on our grass, Tuohy's was all chewed to the butt. Dad always went over to tell him, otherwise he reckoned Tuohy would think we didn't mind.

 The cottage was mostly hidden by a rough box hedge around front and back. I climbed over a stone wall along the side of the field and came into the boreen. Tuohy's Fiesta van was parked down at the end. I went to his gate, but it was covered with the hedge. Tuohy had torn out a tyre sized hole for access. The path inside was cracked and moss-eaten, the green paint on the front door was peeling. I was thinking about whether to shout from the road or climb through the hedge, go up and knock, when I heard the jingle of the 'Death Notices' on the bog road. By the time I got back to the mobile, Ann was parked outside, window down, she drew on her e-fag.

Our Lady tapped the dash as Ann turned and drove up through The Mackon. 'What were you doing in the field?'

'Tuohy's cattle broke in again.'

'Oh dear. Did you get your homework done?'

'We didn't get any, the first day.'

'Hit the ground running, Tommy. Do your work right. Don't do what I did, leave school early and be a skivvy all your life. All those books in the mobile, under the sofas. They're yours, aren't they?'

'They were mam's. When she started studying medicine.'

'Ah, of course.' Ann tapped her e-fag over the ashtray, even though there were no ashes to tap.

I knew something was wrong as soon as we got into town. The bread man's van was parked across the road at The Olde Tree. He was out on the kerb, on his phone, looking across at O'Malley's. The shop was blocked off with blue garda tape, a wall of white plastic blanked the petrol pumps area. Pupils lined the cordon. Gardaí and squad cars were everywhere, two suited men stood talking at the side of the shop.

'Oh Lord, not someone murdered,' Ann said, blessing herself and touching the statue of Our Lady.

I was in the smoking woods at lunchtime, starving without my mini roll, before we knew any more about O'Malley's. Another first year, Lally, joined us.

'ATM Job.' He looked at his phone. '"Gardaí believe the unit was removed by a digger: probably a JCB or rubber duck Hymac"'.

'Nice one.' Marley was nodding. I saw Rebecca pass through the tennis courts. She hadn't answered my message. I wasn't surprised. A hand wrapped around Marley's head.

'Howyee girls,' Maurice said, smiling as we were surrounded by Leaving Certs. Lally ran off. I was cornered at the gorse. I dropped my fag. 'Hope that wasn't you last night, Marley.'

'If it was, we want a share!'

'Wouldn't have the balls, would ya, ya faggot!' Maurice pulled Marley's fags off him and started offering them around.

'You shouldn't have, Jake!'

'Ah, but he insists!' Someone knocked Marley's phone out of his hands.

'You want to watch your phone, scan.'

'No worries, daddy'll buy him another.'

'I bought that myself.' Marley was glaring.

'With stolen money, you little knacker!' Someone whacked Marley on the head, this time he kept his head facing the ground. I stared.

'Hey fucko, what are you looking at?' Fingers gripped and violently twisted my right nipple. When they let go, the pain came in waves. Then they were gone.

'If you're getting Maurice back, you might want to hurry it up,' I said, trying to rub the pain away. Marley picked up his phone, found the crumpled fag box in the dead leaves. There were two broken cigarettes left inside.

'Tomorrow after lunch, Tommy. I'll need a bit of a hand though. We'll have to toss a few classes, alright?'

The day passed quickly, everything was different to the village school, classrooms, teachers, voices, it was faster and louder. Rebecca was at the entrance door before me at home time.

'Sorry about that message,' I said, as I reached her. 'I pressed the wrong buttons.'

'It's cool.'

'Have you—'

Marley banged into me. 'Tommy, did you see this?' He shoved his phone in front of me. On the first year Facebook group, a link had been posted: 'ATM RAID IN BALLINCALTY - WATCH LIVE!!!!' The YouTube logo was below the message. 'It's got the whole thing, I– oh shit!'

Marley ran toward the avenue. I looked back down the corridor and saw Maurice and company coming from the Resource Area. When I turned around Marley was already at the poplar island. Rebecca was getting into her mother's Audi. The Assembly Hall door opened, and Sherlock came out. Maurice and friends walked slowly past me and out toward the avenue. Marley was nearly at the gates. Before Sherlock offered me another lift, I decided to leave.

At the end of the avenue, a shiny 12 BMW swung in and stopped beside me. Top of the range model, huge spoiler, chrome alloys. The window rolled down.

'Howya laddo!' dad grinned at me. 'Get in!'

I opened the door and got in. There was smell of leather and it had a walnut dash with computerised screens.

'Did ya win the lotto?'

'Boss man gave me the loan of it. He's sound. Loaded, the bastard. I'm in love with her. If I get enough of this security work, I'll buy it off him.' Dad swung the car around and out the gates. 'How's the schoolin' going? Getting all the lessons done, are ya?'

'It's only the first few days, dad.'

'I know, son. But start as you mean to go on. Will we get a steak across the road?'

The Olde Tree was quiet on a Tuesday evening. One pensioner sat at the counter. Two Junior Cert lads played pool. Jimmy the barman sat on a stool behind the counter, watching Sky News.

'Turn that off, all the action is in this town, Jimmy!' dad said, as we came into the bar.

Jimmy looked over. 'Ah Joe, hello!' We sat at a table beside the unlit fireplace. 'Do ye want menus?'

'Just throw us out two steaks, Jimmy. Onions, mushrooms, peppered sauce and a couple of Cokes.' Jimmy nodded and went out the back. Dad pulled in to the table, his leg jumping. 'Fair play to Ann for bringing ya. We got a bit held up. One of Midnight's army buds never showed, we had a couple of extra shifts. But it's handy money. Working for lads that is loaded. Music guys.'

Maybe they were famous. Maybe dad could get me tickets. I could bring Rebecca to a concert, get backstage passes. That'd make up for that stupid message. 'Who are the band, dad?'

'I don't know their name, Tommy. Something weird — thank you!' Jimmy's son, another Junior Cert, brought over the cokes, cutlery, napkins. 'I just do their security, you know. I don't get involved in any of that stuff. Pots of money in it. If I get enough hours, we'll be flying.'

'Any more news on that job across the road?' dad said, when Jimmy came back out. I could hear the steaks sizzling in the kitchen.

'They came with a JCB or something. Took the whole thing away. O'Malley is gone bananas.'

'Sure what does he care, it's the bank's loss,' dad said. 'And they don't give a hoot either. The only loser is the insurance companies, the snakes. They're worse than the bookies. Do you know how much me brother-in-law has tossed on horses? Them lot have his Army pension on direct debit every month. Got all his lump sum too.'

Jimmy looked out across the street. 'I'd be doubting O'Malley has cover at all. He was in some tangle a few years ago with the Revenue and insolvency. Up in the High Court. He has to do that forecourt perfect or the shop franchise'll pull out and go down the road to Corcoran's. I don't know he'll manage it.'

'He's not short, he'll cover it.'

'It was only filled Monday. There could have been a couple a hundred grand in it. Sharp men, whoever they were. Pros.'

Dad looked up, smiled. 'City knackers.' He swigged the coke. 'Comin' down here to the country bumpkins, terrorising the place. Bastards. I suppose the cops haven't a clue.'

'Couple of detectives came in here earlier.'

'Columbo types?' Dad laughed.

'They seemed slick enough. But they knew nothing. Asking did we hear anything last night, when this side of the street is nearly all commercial. No one living here now, only a few foreigners renting down the end. Steaks will be just a couple of minutes, lads.'

'The foreigners.' Dad nodded. 'You wouldn't know, Jimmy. They could have been involved. Them fellas have different values.'

Tuohy's cattle were gone when we got back to the mobile. At the end of the field, I saw he had just moved the same stakes to different positions. It was drizzling, the morning muck in the sitting room had turned back to liquid and was pouring out the half-built front doorway in a steady green stream. I got a text as I started my homework. It was Marley: 'What ya think of video?' I looked around for the laptop, but dad had already taken it, he was stretched on the far sofa bed swigging Coke, he'd launched his zombie series. He saw me looking over.

'Get a couple of episodes down before that fool comes calling tonight. You've lessons for doing?'

'Just a few things,' I said, sliding my phone back in the pocket. The geography teacher had been happy with my paragraph on the Ozone. Now we had to write out a list of definitions. I got stuck into my work. After a few minutes, I could have been anywhere, even with the soundtrack of groans and tearing skin in the background.

'Ugh!' dad said after a while, someone was screaming in agony. 'You should give this a go, Tommy!'

'Can't stand zombies. Can you turn it down a bit?'

'It'll be no good without the sound!'

'Do you not have headphones?' Dad's phone vibrated. I got back into my paragraph on global warming.

'Fuck!' dad said, reading from the phone. He clicked on the laptop. The audio played on, but in the Perspex I could see he'd minimised the stream. He was on YouTube. Just before he went full screen, I saw the video title: 'ATM RAID IN BALLINCALTY – WATCH LIVE!!!!'

The video wasn't a security cam, that was clear straight away, with the flash of curtain, the slight shake, and it was in colour. Dad left the volume muted. The groans from trapped humans became the soundtrack. O'Malley's Service Station looked weird in the semi-darkness. I'd only ever seen it in the daytime, buzzing with people filling petrol, getting briquettes, children munching crisps at the entrance, O'Malley scowling on his phone as he zigzagged the gas cylinders. I moved my copybook around so I could get the scene into view.

A truck had pulled up to the side of the street in front of O'Malley's. It was a large flatbed, twelve-wheeler, there was a JCB on the back and a steel container. Two figures got out real quick. I guessed they were male by their build, one tall, the other wide and short. They both wore black clothes and balaclavas. The tall man leapt up on the flatbed, got into the JCB. There was a pause and then a puff of smoke from its long exhaust pipe. The other raider moved a lot slower, rubbing his back as he pulled down two ramps at the end of the flatbed. The JCB rolled off onto the forecourt. It sped across by the petrol pumps, smoke streaming, reached the entrance and the alcove that housed the ATM. The unit was sunk into the wall, steel cladding all around it. Above, there was a small window, with a flower box on the sill.

The bucket of the JCB lifted high, there was another burst of smoke as the metal teeth crashed against the brickwork over the hood, you could hear skin being ripped away by the zombies, blood spilling everywhere, as the bucket pulled away part of the wall. The sill above fell, the flower box hit the bucket on the way down, smashing against the tarmac, compost and flowers scattered everywhere. The bucket chewed the metal surrounds. Part of the cladding was attached to iron brackets, the JCB tugged each one out. The smaller figure looked on from the petrol pumps, turning to the street every couple of seconds. The unit came out of the wall, silver sheets of insulation slid around it. The JCB jerked. The unit was caught in something, one of the brackets, smoke rolled in thick clouds from the exhaust. The driver waved across, the other figure hurried to the steel container on the flatbed, opened the lid. He pulled out what looked like a consaw. He carried it over to the unit, bending under the weight. The driver pointed at the bracket. The smaller figure pulled the consaw cord a few times, smoke rose. He began cutting the bracket, sparks flew up into the night.

Dad's episode was now just one constant sound of low groaning. The show had the record for the least dialogue in broadcasting history. I glanced over, his eyes were locked on the screen. I could have snorted cocaine and he wouldn't have noticed.

The bucket pulled the unit away. The consaw operator dragged the tool back to the flatbed, stopping halfway to adjust his grip, rubbing his back after he returned the tool to the box. The JCB bucket now scooped up the unit, wires dragging underneath, some of the tarmac coming away with it, the whole thing jerked across the forecourt, the bucket then dropped the unit on the flatbed, with bits of tarmac and a few bricks. The JCB moved around to the ramps and rolled back up on the platform. The driver jumped out, hurried off the flatbed, tossed up the ramps. The other raider was already in the cab. The flatbed turned on the road and went up through the town, lights off, towards Cloonloch. The next video started loading: 'WHEN ATM JOBS GO WRONG!!!!'

Dad reached for his Majors. I took out my phone, clicked on YouTube, turned the volume down, careful it didn't reflect in the Perspex. That's the trouble with living in a mobile home, it's like a world of mirrors, everyone can see what you're doing all the time.

Again, I watched the JCB come off the ramps, the consaw firing sparks, the unit full of cash dropped on the flatbed. The whole thing took less than four and a half minutes. Dad had closed the laptop, he was gone outside, on the phone. I could just see his silhouette at the road and the red-hot end of his fag.

Dad was moody next morning. I always knew when he was off. Usually he'd be saying 'Let's go lad,' or 'All right, Tommy?' or 'Where are me poxy fags?' But this morning all I got was grunting. Midnight hadn't come at his usual nine o'clock for their six hours of card playing. But I didn't think that was why dad was in bad form. He never even turned the music centre on as we left The Mackon, although the BMW was still a massive novelty, the smell of plastic, the purr of the engine. In Ballincalty, the forecourt was still cordoned off, but the shop was open. Dad gave me €2 as we stopped just where the truck had during the raid. 'You don't have to wait, I can walk up the avenue, dad.'

'I might not be able to collect you this evening. Could have a job on. Midnight too. I'll give Ann a ring, but I think she has some yoga shite of a Wednesday, he does be raving about having to cook.'

'Midnight has to cook?

'He has to heat up his dinner in the microwave. One of the bogger lads'll give you a lift. There's a pizza in the freezer.'

I got out of the car. 'I don't really know them lads.'

'Don't be thick.'

'Dad, I—'

'Haven't you a poxy tongue in your head? Ask one of them, will ya? And keep at them books!' He drove away without waiting for a reply.

At the shop entrance, I could see in behind the white plastic. One of the suited men from the morning before, the tall bald one, I guessed he was one of the detectives, stood around the hole left by the unit. He looked up as I passed. The usual crowd were swarming inside, the two ladies and O'Malley clicking things through, the owner getting confused with every second order.

'No, three fifty…it's a breakfast roll…this is just a bacon roll? Why does it say breakfast roll then? … Maurice! Maurice!' O'Malley shouted across. 'Is this a bacon roll? … Then why did you put "breakfast roll" on the sticker, huh?'

I went down the aisle to the deli counter. 'Two mini rolls, please.'

'Two? Jesus, Tommy, you're splashing out! You must have stole the ATM, huh? Where's that slag today?' Maurice forked out two mini rolls, tossed them in a paper bag.

'Maurice!' O'Malley shouted across. 'The Brioche!'

We had a double of Art first thing. Mr Coyne walked around the square of chairs and tables, he wore a woollen polo neck, his moustache creased as he spoke, his hands were deep in his corduroy pockets.

'So children, let us begin by asking the question: "What is art?"' Everyone looked around dumbly. I liked the Art & Crafts Room straight away, the different lay out of the class, the smell of paint, the large windows, the abstract shapes in the corner made from cardboard, the overall unusualness of the place. I'd managed to squeeze in beside Rebecca although I couldn't shake off Marley, who jumped in the other side.

'You boy?'

'Sir?' It was Lally.

'What is art?'

'Eh…pictures?'

'Pictures.' Mr Coyne scratched his moustache. 'You mean paintings? Yes. Can you tell me more, though? This girl?' It was Candy Floss Karen.

'It can be sculptures. Or…'. She looked at the pottery wheel. 'Pots…or…maybe, I don't know…films?'

'Very good, yes. So, it comes in different forms, are we agreed?' Everyone nodded slowly. 'But do we only find art in galleries, museums or cinemas? Hmm?' Mr Coyne looked out the windows. 'That scene out there. Those fields, that hill, those trees. Is that art?'

'No,' someone said.

'Who said no?' Mr Coyne looked at Marley. 'You boy? Name?'

'Jake.'

'Why not, Mr Jake?'

'They're just trees. How'd they be art, sir?'

'Interesting.' Mr Coyne sucked in air and walked back up to the top of the room. He sat behind his desk and leant his jaw on his hands. 'What we must take note of now, children, are the three stages of Art. These are the elements of process. That is, the first being "Absorption". You soak up the atmosphere around you. Number 2 is "Meditation". You begin to consider how to project that atmosphere into the way it appears to you.' Someone yawned. Mr Coyne looked around and made a little grimace. 'Before anyone dozes off, let's try and prove Mr Jake wrong, eh class?' Marley scowled. 'We will do some sketches of that scene out there, alright? Doesn't have to be exactly as it is, just whatever way seems right to you. Pencils, sheets at the far window. One sheet at a time please. And only take the 2b pencils, thank you!'

As we started sketching, I angled myself so I could see Rebecca's work. She'd started with just a leaf, so I did the same, we could compare notes after. Suzanne and

39

Karen were giggling the whole time on the other side. I saw they'd just started drawing cocks and balls. Marley had his ruler out, he was making a triangle.

'What the hell is that, Marley?' I said.

'How else am I supposed to get the side of it straight?'

'It's a hill, not one of the Pyramids. Anyway, you don't need to draw anything, we're all proving you wrong, remember?'

'Piss off.'

Rebecca had a leaf sketched.

'Not bad,' I risked. She looked at me, brown eyes hypnotic.

'It's like a duck's foot, Tommy.'

'No, it's good, really.'

'Now, that's good,' she was looking at mine. 'Do you do a lot of drawing?'

'Not really.' She looked at her sheet.

'I can't get it the way I see it in my mind. How do you do it?'

'I just kind of go with it.'

'How do you mean?'

'Don't know. Just let it draw itself or something.' I felt myself going red. One of the children from town had their hands up. Mr Coyne lifted his head from his hands.

'Yes?'

'What's the third one, sir?'

'What's that boy?'

'The third stage. You said there was three…things of process.'

'Good, this is what we are doing now,' Mr Coyne said. 'The final application of the creative idea in the way you see fit. I call this stage "Execution."'

Marley looked over my shoulder. 'That a ball of phlegm, Tommy?' he said. He pulled me back from the table. 'Don't forget that job today,' he was whispering.

'What job?'

'Operation Maurice.'

We smoked at the gorse bush at first break. Lally was focussed on the double doors for Sherlock, while me and Marley scanned the tennis courts and the football pitch behind for any incoming viruses of Maurice and friends.

'That video was class.'

'Ballincalty crime world exposed!'

'I heard them city detectives are using it to trace them now.'

'Where'd ya hear that, Lally? Are you on the Garda Pulse system?'

'Ol' man met O'Malley in the Tree last night.'

'How can they track it?'

'Some numbers they found on the truck. Whoever filmed that has really screwed them boys.'

'Who'd be out at that time though?' I said.

'Watch it!' Marley said, dropping the fag. I saw the bullet head of Sherlock pan around the tennis courts. We hurried deeper into the greenery, other smokers noticed us and flashes of blue began to retreat from the bushes toward the football pitch, hundreds of dying fag butts tossed quickly to the withering leaves.

We had got into a routine of going to the Resource Area at lunchtime. We sat along the walled line of seats, chewing on sandwiches, crisps and drinking minerals. The town kids were allowed go home, or to the shops. Rebecca and some other girls sat across from us. I swallowed the last of my mini roll as Marley got up, tossing his schoolbag to one side.

'Come on for a smoke, Tommy,' he said, mayonnaise on his chin.

'I'm still sick after that couple at first break.'

'You're no good. Lally?' Lally got up sleepily. 'Meet me here at five to two, alright?' Marley said, turning for the doors.

'What about history?' I said.

'You don't go to it, scan.'

I watched them go past the V.P., through the exit and up the steps to the tennis courts. I balled up the shop packet and tossed it at the bin. It bounced off the lid, rolled over to a pair of feet. Rebecca's.

'Oops. Sorry,' I said as she looked up from her phone. For once Carrot Head Suzanne or Candy Floss Karen weren't chewing her ear off.

'That bin isn't for recycling, Tommy.'

'Is it not?'

'You have to use the one upstairs.' She went back to her phone.

'Where's that? What difference does it make?' I went over and picked up the paper. She looked up.

'It's the environment.'

'But I don't know where the bin is?' She groaned and got up.

'Follow me.' I walked up the stairs after her. We got to the entrance doors.

'Right there,' she nodded at a green bin. I tossed the paper in. She walked back toward the Resource Area.

'Do you want to take a run down the shops?' I called after her. 'Sherry Trifle doesn't know who the townies are yet.'

'Huh?' she stopped at the stairs, turned, blonde strands swinging. 'I'd say he knows you're not one of them. But okay.'

I couldn't believe it, we walked out together through the front parking area, around the poplar island with the other town kids. I was happy, but the gaps of silence were awful.

'Got your history done?' I managed. It was a bit of an own goal though, as her response was so detailed, and I hadn't a clue what she was on about. I'd been so excited after watching the ATM video the night before, I couldn't settle at homework and started looking at fast cars online. As she talked about visiting local archaeological sites, a bird landed just ahead of us on the avenue, poking its beak at a piece of tossed crust.

'Isn't he lovely? Very tame,' Rebecca said and smiled at me. The bird was mostly black feathered, but I didn't think it was a crow, it had flecks of grey and white. It picked up tiny pieces of the bread with the beak. I gazed at the narrow orange legs holding up the body. 'Can you draw wildlife, Tommy?'

'Don't know.'

'Could you draw him?'

'I'd say it'd be hard.'

'Give it a go next class.'

Our hands brushed as we neared the gates. A few fourth years came the opposite way, made kissy noises as they passed. Rebecca made no reaction and neither did I. It was a relief to get to the street, keeping conversation up was harder than endless laps of the football pitch.

There was a dirty red van parked in O'Malley's forecourt. All the Garda tape and sheets had been taken away. A heavy man squeezed into a check shirt and jeans, measuring tape hooked at his waist, tapped a trowel against the side of the hole left by the unit. A younger man wheeled out a small cement mixer. A pile of sand had been tipped beside some bricks.

'Do you want an ice cream, Rebecca?'

'You're gonna buy me an ice cream, Tommy?'

'Why not?' I said. She laughed. This was a good sign. The shop was busy, the townies queued up at the deli counter, deep fat fryers were sizzling, kids got plastic trays of curry chips, chicken burgers, sausages. O'Malley had moved across the shop, he too wore an apron now. He stood next to Maurice, their foreheads damp with sweat.

'The sausages, Maurice, the sausages! Will you get them out of the oven? Now! Wake up, will ya!' One of O'Malley's staff served me two 99s. I paid with the fiver Ann had given me. We sat on the brick wall outside the pumps and ate our ice-creams, right where the raiders had parked.

'You're as mad as a brush, Tommy O'Toole.'

'You got some on your chin there.' She looked at me. I felt heat on my face. She pulled out her phone, clicked on 'Mirror', wiped it off with a tissue she had pulled from somewhere. I could have sat forever watching the traffic zoom by, people tied up in the busyness of the day. I'd never want to be any of them, or the staff in the shop, or the other kids, or the teachers in the school or anyone, anywhere else, there was nowhere I'd rather have been then on that wall, just the two of us, chilling.

Rebecca finished off her cone. 'So you heard about the lunchtime disco Friday?'

'A disco? At lunchtime?'

'Everyone is going. It's going to be—'

'The lovebirds!' Marley and his cheese and onion breath dived between us. 'Does Sherry Trifle know Mr and Mrs O'Toole are out on the town?' Rebecca made a face. Maybe she just didn't like the surname 'O'Toole'. 'It's only us city slickers allowed through the gate for lunch privies! Move over there, boss!' Marley pushed between us and sat down. 'Tommy buy you an ice cream? And all the fags I'm givin' him?'

Rebecca had stood up. 'It's nearly two, we'd want to be getting back.' She took up her schoolbag, swung it around her shoulder. I got up and followed her. Marley kept talking to me, but all I could hear was the humming cement mixer being filled with shovelfuls of sand behind us on the forecourt.

45

As we got to the avenue gates, Marley pulled my arm toward one of the pillars. Rebecca walked ahead of us, her blonde strands bouncing gently on her shoulders. 'Let her off, scan.'

'Why?'

'Don't want her seeing where we're going.'

'And where is that? She was just asking me about the disco when you came.'

'Asking you what? It's just a school lunchtime thing. Pure shite. Teachers'll be everywhere. There. Now you know all about it.'

'She was asking me.'

'But you didn't know anything, did ya?'

I took a deep breath. 'I thought we were meeting up in the Resource Area?'

'This saves time. We're going down here.' I looked beyond his arm.

'Jake, that's a fence. And that's a field.'

'It's a shortcut to the Golf Club.'

'What are you on about?'

'Come on, time is ticking.'

We climbed the fence, ran across the field, behind O'Malley's, a few large houses along the street, then the town square. Despite everything, it was exciting, out of bounds during school hours. We scaled a cut stone wall, came onto a winding gravel drive. Up at the end, there was a carpark and a clubhouse. Marley took out a key and opened the glass entrance door. He led me down a shiny wooden floored hall. We passed glass displays of silver cups and shields, photos of smiling golfers, some in school uniforms. We came into a large cream kitchen. 'Do you play golf?'

'Ol' lad goes the odd time. They have him cleaned out with green fees every year for all he comes. Cup of tea?' He opened one of the presses, took out two mugs stamped with the club emblem.

'Marley, what are we doing here?'

'Waiting.'

'Waiting for what?'

'For the guy. He said he'd be here between two and three and not to be late.'

'What guy is this?

'You'll see.'

We had a cup of golf clubhouse tea and went outside for a couple of smokes. I didn't inhale all the time, they were making me dizzy. Marley kept talking about stuff he'd seen on the internet, he watched things all night by the sound of it, reality beheadings, live torture, porn of course, all sorts of crazy shit. At about quarter to three, a 12 Vectra came up the drive fast. It stopped in front of us. The window rolled down. The driver was in a black t-shirt, he had curly dark hair and a goatee.

'Ho-aye, scan?' Marley said, real casual. The man looked out the window.

'What the fuck's this?' We heard him reach for his door handle.

'We just want to—'

'I'll break your legs!'

'Hang on, boss,' Marley pulled out a yellow two hundred euro note, his hand was shaking. The man sat back in his seat, glaring.

'Roll that up, you tit!'

Marley squeezed the money in his fist.

'What do yiz girls want all that for?'

'Party.'

'If I hear stuff is moving outside of me you're fucking dead!'

'No way. Nothing like that.'

'Get over here.' I couldn't see the exchange. The car wheels spun as the Vectra moved off, down the drive toward the street.

'What a personality.'

'You're not going smoking that?'

'Not likely. Let's get out of here.' Marley pushed the fag-box-sized package into his boxers and we went back over the stone wall, across the large field, turned up parallel with the avenue and went around by the old convent building. At the back, we could hear voices from the football pitch.

'There must be training,' I said. I saw flashes of players, heard the bounce of a ball.

'I'm banking on it. Leaving Cert team. Maurice plays in midfield.'

'How d'ya know?'

'I did my homework. Now we need to get in there. Do you think we're still covered by that line of trees along the path?' I looked at the green door where Maurice and company had flung us out.

'Why?'

'We're going down to the changing rooms.'

'You're not going planting all that stuff on him, are you? He'll get sent off to one of those detention cetres or something. Jail if he's eighteen.'

'Ten out of ten.'

'The father'll go bananas. He'll have a heart attack at the shop counter.'

'Exactamundo. Sale and supply. I know the law, scan. Come on.'

We crept down along the old convent wall, still in the cover of the trees. We went in the side door and ran along the flaking corridors, the memory of being hauled through still fresh. We came out in the courtyard, passed the Wet Room and down another hallway.

'You know your way around here.'

'I scoped the place early this morning.'

'Must have been early.'

'Six bells. I told you I'm an insomniac. Ol' lad as well. Two of us up watching shite on our laptops the whole night.'

'You're keen to get him.'

'He spat in my face and then he stuck my head in a pot of his own piss. Kind of encourages you.'

'What if someone comes?'

'Why would anyone?

49

'Lally reckons Sherlock is lurking all over the school during the day looking for smokers.' Marley opened the changing room door.

'Fuck Lally! Ah, shit. It's all lockers.' We stood inside. Lockers lined the walls, there were benches across the middle. Everyone's stuff was safe behind small golden padlocks. There was a smell of sweat, socks, chlorine from the showers beyond.

'Didn't check this?'

'The changing rooms were locked.'

'Let's get out of here, Jake.'

'That hall leads out to a door to the pitch and up to the Resource Area. You stand down at the corner and watch for Sherry.' Marley had a short piece of coat hanger wire out.

'What's that for?'

'I'm gonna open them and find Maurice's.'

'Where'd you learn how to do that?'

'Are you mad? Wikihow, where else?' There were footsteps out in the hall. Distant, but approaching.

'Sherlock,' I whispered.

'Behind the lockers.'

'No, he'll check that. The showers.'

Two first years getting caught in the changing rooms during Leaving Cert practice would not go down well with the Principal. The Leaving Certs might not be too impressed either. There was also the large amount of hash in Marley's boxers, although it wasn't likely that Sherlock would want a look in there. We went into the communal wash room. It was a large tiled area of showers. There was nowhere to hide. We'd have been better off behind the lockers. The footsteps came closer, near the changing room door. We stood against the tiled wall. I was afraid my breathing could be heard. The footsteps stopped, the handle turned. The door opened, the footsteps entered the changing room. Leather shoes. The door closed. Silence.

'He's gone.' It was like a dream, we'd escaped.

'Hold on.' I pulled Marley's arm. 'How do you know he doesn't stall out there in the hall until the lads come back? We'll walk straight into him!' Marley looked across at a line of small rectangular windows.

'Let's try them.'

We spent ten minutes painfully squeezing out through the frames. I scraped my hip on the catches. The screen of trees was riskily thin this far down the path. As I landed, I heard a whistle blown, training was over. We crept back to the field. The whole time I expected someone who'd spotted us through the trees to shout up from the pitch. I breathed deeply as we got to the trees along the avenue.

'We'll get the bastard tomorrow morning,' Marley said, lighting up.

'Give us one. How?'

'At the deli counter. He always brings his schoolbag to work.'

'In the shop? But I thought you were barred?'

'Don't worry about that,' Marley said. 'We need to get off-site right now. You can come back to mine until four if you want.'

'Nah, I'll cross here over to the bog road. I've no lift, I better start walking.'

'I think your man in the Vectra was going out to the bog, Tommy. You could have asked him for a lift!'

The road to The Mackon was dead silent. I liked the quietness. Part of me didn't want anyone to come. I could just stand at the ditch, looking out across the field, beyond the chewing cattle, sheep tearing tiny bundles of grass, to the specks of houses, the mountains. There was a rattle. Tuohy's van had stopped at least two hundred yards before it reached me. I'd probably have been quicker walking, but I got in anyway. Local radio blared, there was a smell of calf nuts and cow shite. A picture of Padre Pio was glued to the dash. Tuohy stared at me as I looked around for the seatbelt. He wore a spattered Champion top, a peaked cap with 'Boston Crowbars' across the front.

'Howya Jack. Nice day.' He sucked on a chupa-chup as he clutched with a huge green wellington, the gears crushed and we moved off.

Dad's BMW was parked at the mobile. As I got inside, I heard the shower running. There was a strange perfume. On my sofa bed, a slender woman wearing only heels scrolled on her phone. She was maybe in her twenties, with light brown skin. I stared at her nipples, then at the floor. She looked up. I turned to her again, tried to focus on her face, dark curls over her shoulders.

'Hi honey!' she said, in a foreign accent, as she reached for my blanket, covering her breasts.

'Who's that?' dad shouted from the shower. My face was hot. I turned and went back out, shut the door. I sat in the back seat of the BMW and started my homework.

Rats raced across the cracked vinyl tiles. Dad was in the back garden. His face was strained as he shoved connected chimney sweep pipes up the sewer drain. Turds floated around in our toilet bowl. Me and mam sat at the long kitchen table looking at new house plans. Birds landed in front of us. They were black with flecks of grey and white, with real thin legs. They pecked at the plans, tearing bits off in their tiny beaks.

I threw off the blanket, sweat all over me. Midnight lay across on the far sofa bed, his socked foot hanging out over the end, sand boots tossed on the floor. There were playing cards, empty cans of Dutch Gold and Coke, fag and cigar butts scattered all over the table. Dad slept in his double bed beyond the cooker. There was a noise, it seemed like outside movement. It could have been heavy footsteps. I got up, leant across Midnight, looked out through the Perspex. The panel was damp, but it had stopped raining. I wiped away the condensation. Moonlight gave a blue hue to everything. The noises weren't Tuohy's cattle out late for a stroll, the field was empty. I pulled on my jeans and runners, went outside. I took out one of the loose fags Marley had given me, lit up, coughed. I walked around the back of the mobile. Something was crossing the fence at the end of the field, but I couldn't see if it was a fox or a person. The grass was soaked, blades dropped water inside my runners. The stones around Ash's grave were like a perfect smile. The clouds moved, killing the moonlight. The smile melted into the darkness.

Dad stood in his boxers, turning sausages with a fork, a cigarette in his mouth, ashes falling in cubes onto the scalding cooking oil, spattering in the pan. 'Let's go, Tommy! Midnight! Come on!'

Midnight groaned. 'For the love of God, is it morning already?' His nose was blocked, I could tell by his voice.

'It is and we need to get moving. We're meeting him at half nine.' He looked at me as I buttoned up my shirt. 'No uniform today, Tommy. I'll give you a pass. Meself and Mid need a hand.'

'Yeah, good idea, Joe, my back is giving out.'

'Your back can give out all it wants. Tommy is a lookout, that's it. Pock is stripping and I'm cutting. You're on the barrow and drag, Private.'

'If I end up on me end—'

'You can pick yourself up out of the muck!' Dad brought over three plates of sausages and sat beside me on the sofa bed.

The block layers had most of the ATM hole built up. One of them scraped his trowel along the mortar joints in the top line of bricks. Another filled sand into the turning mixer drum.

'O'Malley is not wasting any time,' Midnight said, as we passed.

'He has no choice according to Jimmy in the Tree. Franchises are onto him. If he doesn't get it back in shape quick, they'll pull out. I'll get them boys to come and price my place.'

'You goin' at it again?'

'I want it roofed by Christmas. We'll be out of that sardine can by Paddy's day.'

'That a good idea, Joe, so quick? I mean with the car an' all?'

'It's this security stuff, Midnight, this security work that we're getting. It'll cover it, alright?'

'Oh yeah, yeah.'

It was exciting to think of our house finally being built. I knew all the rooms marked out by the stub walls, the kitchen-diner, the sitting room, front hall, master bedroom, my own room. I'd often imagined how it would look, where I'd put all my books and stuff, if I'd have a desk for doing homework.

I saw Marley come up through the town. There was a bounce to his walk, he was going in for the kill, but he'd have to wait another day at least, unless he went on a solo run. I sent him a text: 'Held up with my dad'. He didn't answer.

A little way out the Cloonloch road we turned off onto a one-lane track, which ran for miles up a gradual hill. We passed through a woody valley and along sparse hilly ground, we were coming back into bog land. We came to the boreen which led up to The Castle. It was no more than a three-bed bungalow, but locals called it The Castle due to its views of Ballincalty, The Mackon and the landscape for many miles. We passed by two cracked pillars at the gateless entrance. We parked at the side of the house. Around the back, there were a few whitewashed outhouses, with asbestos roofs and galvanised double doors. A 13 Audi was parked at one. The driver sank low in his seat, his round head set deep in his shoulders, owl-like eyes over a thick ginger moustache. He was staring at The Castle. Dad's family home burnt down in the early 1980s when he was seven or eight. My grandparents suffocated during the blaze. Dad managed to escape. Only the four walls remained, greenery had all but covered the soot. 'What are we doing here, dad?'

We hadn't been out there for years. I'd heard dad tell Midnight he didn't even own The Castle anymore, something to do with the bank. 'Just taking apart a bit of industrial shite, lad. Old air conditioning units, stuff like that. Dumping them into the swamp. The fella is giving us a few quid, saves him a lot. That's our security boss, over there. Midnight's old quartermaster.'

'So he's Pock—'

'Jesus Christ, Paddy, Paddy is his name,' Midnight said, bursting into a bout of coughing. He pulled out a roll of toilet paper, blew his nose. 'Fuckin' hell. If he hears you calling him that he'll shoot me. Pure head case.'

Dad turned to me. 'Give me your phone and take mine, Tommy. There's credit on it. Go down to them pillars. If you see anyone coming, give me a ring, alright?'

'Who'd be coming?'

'Eco-warriors, son. Green men. If they see us, they'll cause shite. Fines and all sorts, you know? But here you'll be able to see them coming for miles.' They got out and went over to Pock. I turned and walked down toward the pillars. I sat on a flat part of the ditch. I logged onto dad's internet. Rebecca had sent me a Facebook message: 'Going to Lunch Disco tomorrow?'

Result!

As I typed 'Deffo!', a small engine throbbed from behind The Castle. Then the consaw roared. There was hammering. After a few minutes, sparks flew around the gable. The galvanised doors swung open.

Soon, a black cloud rose to the sky. I saw Midnight slowly dragging pieces of scrap metal to the deep bog swamp at the back of The Castle. I played fruit games for a while. Then, when I got bored scrolling through endless Facebook posts, I went on National Geographic and read a bit about global warming. The geography teacher would have been proud of me. Dad brought down a can of Coke and a Mars bar to me at twelve.

'Nearly there, son. Just tidying up.'

I tore into the goodies and went back to global erosion issues. It was almost three when they were finished. There was a smell of oil and burning rubber. The Audi passed by first, Pock ignored me as he zoomed down the road. Midnight's jeep was followed by dad. He was covered in rust and oil. My phone buzzed as I got in the BMW. A text had finally come from Marley: 'Shop early'.

The country and western music was louder than usual as we walked up the corridor at St. Michael's. I knew most of the staff to see, they smiled at me and nodded as I passed them. Nora grabbed my arm as we went into the ward.

'Gerald? Gerald?' She looked at me, smiling.

'Sorry…eh…'.

'I'm going home today.' Her smile faded. 'You're not Gerald, are you?'

'He's not and you're not,' dad said in a growl, as we went down to the end of the ward. I pulled my arm away. The other woman lay across from mam in her bed, the blanket still pulled up around her chin, her eyes tightly shut. I wondered had she moved at all since the last time I was there. Mam was sitting by the window. Dad sunk into the visitor's chair. I leant against the radiator.

'Hi, mam.'

'You alright, Sheila?'

'Pat?' Nobody said anything for a good few minutes. The music had been turned down. You could hear the wipe of a mop out in the corridor, smell Flash.

'I'm going home this evening,' Nora said from the other side of the ward, she had sat down again.

'Pat?' Mam tightened her hands on her lap. Dad's knees were hopping. He tapped the side of the bed. He felt around in his jacket, took out his Majors.

'I'm going out for a fag. We'll go then, Tommy. You probably have lessons for doing.'

Not really, as I hadn't been at school, but I nodded. I watched him ignore Nora's question as he went out. I looked out the window for a while, at the neatly cut green areas, the yellowing leaves of the trees. Mam made a little groan.

'Who's Pat, mam?' I said it without thinking and straight away wished I hadn't. It was like I was being cheeky, as if I was asking a magician how he did his tricks. I looked at mam, she met my eyes for a moment. I thought then it would have been great, if for once she got clear, if she knew what I asked, what was real and what wasn't. Like if she really knew there was no one she knew called Pat, or maybe she could tell me who she meant by Pat. I wanted to understand what she was saying, what she wanted me to know. I hated that, that I couldn't, that nobody seemed to be able to understand her and she couldn't understand anyone and she was alone.

She looked at me, sort of smiled. There was a splash on the floor. A pool grew under mam's chair.

'Mam, no, don't do that!' I went to the double doors, brushed past Nora's outstretched arm. One of the carers I'd met on the way in was still in the hall doing something at a trolley. 'Eh, miss?

'What is it, sweetheart?' She came to the door.

'It's my mother, she...'. The carer went in.

'Sheila, what are you doing?' I went out to find dad in the gazebo.

I was in the big kitchen. There was a hole in the window. Wind blew in. A butcher's calendar hung crookedly on the wallpapered wall. There was a pool of water on the vinyl tiles. Footsteps moved around overhead. Mam stood at the range. She mashed potatoes in a little pot. I could smell smoke. I heard the tapping of a hammer. Mam stopped mashing and looked at the chimney. I saw a ladder outside the window. My Ben 10 toy fell over on the floor. The tapping on the roof got louder.

I opened my eyes. Midnight lay across from me, mouth wide open, can in one hand, he was snoring. It was half four on my phone. The tapping noise continued. It was something outside. I got up, leant across my uncle, wiped the Perspex. I could just see the toothy smile of stones around Ash's grave. There was a chill, the door of the mobile wasn't fully closed. I looked over at dad's bed. It was empty.

Dad kept hopping channels on the music centre as we drove to Ballincalty next morning. There'd be a minute of current affairs, then rap music, a clip of classical and back to the politics. Eventually he shut it off and we got to town in silence. He pulled up at the short wall outside O'Malley's. The ATM hole was all bricked up. The new unit was going to be in-store. Dad waved over at the block layers as they wheeled their mixer and barrows into the red van. I saw Marley coming down the street. 'I'll get a price off these fellas,' dad said, pulling the handbrake.

'I'll get out here for a sausage roll. Do you have €2, dad?' Dad handed me the coin and grabbed my arm as I got up.

'Things are gonna change for us now, Tommy. I'll get these lads to finish off the block laying. We'll be out of that poxy mobile home by Paddy's day, you'll see. You'll have your own room, and your own desk for doing all your lessons, alright? The fella was fair happy with us getting rid of all that scrap for him. He's giving us a ton of security hours.' Dad got out and went into the forecourt. Marley had stopped at the short wall.

'What happened yesterday?'

'I had to help dad and my uncle get rid of some rubbish.'

'We'd some rubbish here needed getting rid of an' all. Me and Lally got jumped again in the woods at lunchtime.'

'Shit.'

'It's past time to get this done.'

'So I distract Maurice asking something about the sausage rolls, while you put the stuff in his bag?'

'No. I was thinking about it last night. If O'Malley sees me in the shop, he's goin' to start quacking straight away. It'll be better if I cause the disruption. Everyone'll be watching me, while you plant the gear.'

'Me? Me plant it?'

'Look, it's easy, scan.' Marley turned to the window. 'See in there at the meat slicing yoke. That's Maurice's bag hanging up. It's got one of them pencil pouch yokes no one ever uses. Just stick it in there. It'll be on him then. I'll get the cops onto it, and he'll be screwed.'

'I don't know, Jake. It sounds like you're going a bit too far.'

'Wet Room too far, you mean? Didn't stop them pricks, did it?' Marley took out a bag of Hunky Dorys. 'Slip the stuff out of this when you get around the display.' Inside the crisp bag, I could see the packet, tightly wrapped up.

'But what if he sees me? They'll probably do me for selling it. It's a lot of stuff, you said so yourself.' Marley looked around, the shop was getting busy with pupils. I just wanted to get my sausage roll and get up to double art at nine o'clock.

'Chillax, will ya. No one'll see you. They'll all be watching me. I'll make sure of it.'

'This is stupid. Why don't you just go up and tell Sherlock about all this shite in the woods and the Wet Room. Isn't that what he's there for? I'm sure he'd do something about it.'

'You're not...'. Marley looked appalled. 'You're not telling me to squeal, are you, Tommy? I can fight my own battles. I don't need the Sherry Trifle to step in.'

'Are you not going to the cops, though?'

'Anonymously.'

'What's the difference?'

'Big difference.' Marley grabbed the crisp bag. 'If you don't want to do it, fine. I'll get Lally, fuck ya. His ears are still red from yesterday.' Marley took out his phone. I saw it all playing out. Marley distracting O'Malley and Maurice, Lally planting the dope with ease, the celebrations of suffering first years as Maurice was handcuffed and shoved into the back of a squad car in front of the whole school, me looking on at the back of the crowd.

'Give it to me.' I pulled the bag back. 'I'll do it.'

The block layers and dad had driven off. We went in the sliding doors. Marley turned right, passed by a long queue at the tills.

'You're barred, Marley!' I heard O'Malley, as I went across to the far aisle, down by the dairy fridges and toward the deli counter. Marley had stopped opposite Maurice. He held two doughnuts up to his ears. He squeezed them, jam dripped on the floor. Maurice glared.

'Hey Mo, these might work?'

'You're barred, you little prick.'

'You don't have a brain under that yellow cock of hay? But one of these jammy doughnuts might do the trick? Just stick them in your earhole! Or is your brain down in your arse? You know what to do so!' Maurice came around the counter. Marley waved at him, backing quickly up the aisle, tossing the doughnuts on the floor. It would not be good for Marley if his plan didn't work out. O'Malley tried to get across the shop, but there was now a crowd in his way. I looked around, everyone was watching the show. I went by the deli counter, pulled the stuff out of the crisp bag. At the back of the ham slicer, I found the schoolbag. I flicked open the lapel of the pencil pouch, pushed the gear deep into it, flicked the lapel back on. I kept my eyes on the tiles as I went back by the dairy fridges.

I tried to make the underside of the bird look as if it was breathing in as it landed on a bed of leaves. There was a buzz from it, I didn't really know why, making action appear on a blank sheet. 'That's quite competent, Tommy,' Mr Coyne said, from over my shoulder. 'Have you done much drawing before first year?'

'Not really, sir.'

'Hmm. You've managed a fair representation of movement there. Good lad. Keep it up.'

Rebecca looked over when Mr Coyne was gone. The seating arrangements in the Art Room had worked in my favour. Everyone had kept positions from the first class. In all the other rooms, Rebecca was up the top, me and

Marley down the back. She wore a different perfume today, or maybe it was her shampoo, she chewed gum.

'Cool Tommy. It's like that bird we saw the last day.'

'That's what I was trying. I thought about making it pick up a bit of bread with its beak. Bit tricky though.'

'Next time, maybe. How'd you get the feathers so detailed?'

'Kind of outlined them a good bit first. Light with the pencil. If it's not too dark, it's easy change it around if you need to, once you know where you are.'

'God, I thought it was enough to draw it once. Sounds too much like hard work. You going to the disco at lunch?'

'Deffo.' For once, Marley hadn't dived in between us. He scanned his phone every time Mr Coyne was busy. I guessed he was searching for any news of a schoolboy arrested for drug dealing.

Yellow, red and green lights sprayed everywhere in the Assembly Hall. The blinds had been drawn. The maths teacher was on supervision, he scrolled on his phone at the door. As I walked in, I could see flashes of teenage faces on the floor, blue collars looked silver, I saw snatches of golden glitter, banned purple eyeshadow, earrings. I could smell deodorant and afternoon sweat. The prefects had organised a DJ, who had set up on the stage. He jerked, his hands on huge Sony headphones.

'Let's puuuump it uuuup!' The first years were in the far corner. I pushed through dancers. Maurice stood over me, a huge dark shape.

'It's Gerry Sweeney's rent boy!' He twisted my nipple, someone else smacked me across the head. Marley was lying low, refusing to go to the disco, with the Deli King still roaming freely. I got away from them in the crowds of dancers. At the other end of the hall, I found Rebecca. She was leaning against a radiator between Candy Floss Karen and Carrot Head Suzanne.

'Hi! Good disco!' I shouted, my head still stinging. She smiled, then said something I couldn't hear. Her friends backed away a little. I was getting excited by the music, the lights. 'Goin' dancing?' I risked. We were on the floor, our fingers touched. I don't know if it was by accident. Her skin was very soft. We found a space and danced for a few minutes. She was a bit taller than me. I could feel the eyes of her friends on us. She must have too and she guided me by arm towards the end of the hall, to the space under the balcony. Table tennis matches were usually played here at lunchtime, but the tables had been folded away. The Leaving Cert prefects had lined the area with chairs.

'Let's get everyone puuuumping!' The DJ leapt around the stage like he was possessed. We sat near some other kids. I saw a crack of light around the blinds. I realised in a panic the disco would soon be over. We would go back out into the blinding daylight, down to double science in the cold lab, where I sat miles away from Rebecca. As we moved on our seats, her hand brushed against my elbow. I wondered if we were now a couple. It was dark, I could only see her face in the flashes of disco colours. The horror of the national anthem arrived.

Everyone else stood, hands behind their backs, even the DJ was still.

Rebecca turned to me, just as I started to get up. She pulled my arm, reached over and kissed me on the lips. It was nice, a touch, like she felt I was worth kissing, worth knowing, worth the time we'd spent together.

Seconds later we were separated in the crowd as we moved across to the exit.

I stood at the entrance door. The fingers of my left hand were curled in between Rebecca's. We were definitely a couple. Marley was outside, frowning as he looked down the avenue through his phone. 'Are you recording?' I said.

'Course. It'll be online straight after. It'll be perfect for a meme this. I told them four would be a good time. That's probably the hold-up.' The carpark was jammed with cars and buses. I kept an eye on the Resource Area stairs for Maurice. 'There's your old lad, Tommy, in that snazzy motor,' Marley said. I looked down the avenue, saw Dad's BMW sweeping up through the poplars. Rebecca pecked me on the cheek.

'Facebook me later,' she whispered.

'Young love,' I heard Maurice, as a fist connected with my ribs. He and his friends had come out of the Assembly Hall. Sherlock was never around when you needed him. Marley had already disappeared behind thed Principal's Vectra, parked as usual right at the entrance.

'Is that the Guards?' Rebecca said, as I rubbed my side. A squad car was coming up the avenue, blue lights flashing. It was happening. Maurice was going down. I looked at him, he twitched his leg as he tried to get through a crowd of country kids trying to get on their bus. Dad's car swung round the poplar island and pulled up. I acted like I didn't see him. I wanted to watch what happened next with Maurice and the cops. The squad car stopped at the buses. Four guards got out.

'Tommy, let's go,' dad shouted from the driver's window, as he lit a fag. Only now he looked back at the squad car. Maurice had stopped at the end of the bus crowd, the guards came toward him. Marley stood at Sherlock's car. I saw he'd zoomed in on Maurice and the four cops, his tongue almost hanging out.

When I looked down again, the cops had passed by Maurice. He turned, watching, maybe as puzzled as I was. The guards stopped at dad's BMW.

'Step out of the car, please,' the first one said at the driver's window. Dad stared at him. The guard opened the door, another was getting in the passenger side. The guard behind looked in the back, I saw sergeant stripes on his sleeve.

'Let's go, Joe,' the sergeant said.

'What's all this?'

'Your own town, Joe, your own town.'

'Fuck you lot!' Dad tried to pull his door closed, but the guard in the passenger seat shoved him out. Dad disappeared for a second under the blue uniforms. Then there was a flash of handcuffs, they clicked on dad's wrists. He was pushed to the ground, face against tar, eyes darting. The cigarette had rolled to the concrete kerb, still burning.

The place had gone quiet, the only sounds were the Audi ticking over, dad struggling on the ground, the clink of handcuffs. A door closed behind me then, there were footsteps. I saw in the corner of my eye Sherlock stepping outside. But I didn't look around. I just focussed on the glint of silver on dad's wrists until they disappeared into the back of the squad car. Rebecca's mother had stopped behind the squad car. Rebecca let go of my hand. I wondered if she was blushing, if Marley was still filming. I swung my bag on my back and, head down, hurried past the poplar roundabout and out the avenue.

The block layers had taped a quotation to the door of the mobile. I heated a tin of beans, grilled some bread. I turned on the gas heater, it was colder now in the evenings. I took out my *Text & Tests 1*, started my weekend homework. My phone was beeping, there were several text messages, Facebook notifications. I turned the phone off. After I'd done a couple of maths exercises, I pulled out my homework diary. The list was long: geography, English, history, business studies. But I couldn't think straight and soon I tossed the diary onto the far sofa bed.

I turned on the laptop, launched a game Marley had pirated for me. You could create your own town, set out the streets as you wanted, plan municipal buildings, shopping centres, schools. You could even knock forests, drop in houses, choose brick or plaster walls, slate or tile roofs. At some stage, I heard something outside. I looked out through the Perspex. The field was clear of Tuohy's cattle, his latest fencing effort looked to be holding up for the moment. A fox or something had burrowed around Ash's grave. I went out, found the spade in the site. I levelled off the clay, made sure all the stones were back in position.

On the way back inside, I tore the quote off the door, tossed it in the bin. I restarted the game. I finished off a large convenience store in my suburb. I scrolled to aerial view. The place looked detailed, expensive, organised. I attached a sign to the shopfront and saved it.

The waiter polished wine glasses at the dark walnut unit. The glass made a soft dull sound as he twisted the rolled-up cloth around the bulb. Classical music played. Tables were neatly laid with silver cutlery and glasses, pressed white cloth and red napkins, shiny brass candlesticks in the centre. Most of the candles were lit. Flames tossed shadows against orange wallpaper. The dining area was decorated with paintings of rural Italian landscapes, fogged glass panels and diamond-shaped pigeon holes of wine bottles.

'My man! Some more peppered sauce over here.' A speck of mash fell from Marley's lip as he clicked his fingers at the waiter. 'How's that goin' down, Tommy? Steak cooked alright?'

'Are you sure that yoke is okay out there?'

'Will you stop asking me that?' Marley swigged his wine. He coughed. 'The plates,' he said, lowering his voice.

'Yeah, but...if they check them. Run them through that Pulse system—'

'Ah, stop on about your poxy Pulse system, will ya?'

'They'll see they don't exist. Or that they belong to a school bus or something.'

'Why would they bother checking our number plates?'

'What if we meet a checkpoint? '

'Saturday night. Nine o'clock. No checkpoints. Ever. I've done the research. The clever bird catches the worm.'

'It's early.'

'What?'

'The early bird catches the worm.' The waiter was back at the table with a steaming silver jug. 'Some fresh peppercorn sauce, sir.'

'Lovely. Lash her on there, scan. Get me some more of this vino, will ya?'

'Certainly, sir. Was it a Sauvignon Blanc or Chardonnay?'

'It was white, scan.'

'Chardonnay, I think he got,' I said.

'Ho-aye, scan,' Marley squirted a speck of peppered sauce across the table. 'Do you hear the connoisseur? Far from poxy Chardonnay you were reared, hah?' The waiter went to the wine press.

'I tell ya, Tommy,' Marley dabbed his mouth with the tablecloth. 'We're in with the right boys now. Take out my start-up money, we've made a nice whack since the start of the summer.'

'Pity we haven't any of it left.'

'Easy come easy go. We won't bother goin' into the city after this time. Fuck them dirty casinos and tit clubs.

The pimple on that one's arse the last night!' He shook his head. 'We'll just get the night bus straight. Alright?'

'Makes sense.'

'We'll be millionaires before we're eighteen.'

'We might be collared before we're sixteen.'

'I am sixteen, smart lad.' The waiter filled Marley's glass. Marley downed half it.

'Where's he gone?' He looked around a few minutes later. 'He's obsessed with polishing them glasses!'

'What the hell do you want now?'

'Dessert menu.'

'Dessert? Do you not think we'd want to be going? We've another hour and a half to drive?'

'Chillax, scan.' Marley smiled and waved at the waiter.

We zoomed toward the city at a hundred and twenty K on the big road. The yellow of the motorway lights mixed with the blue hue of the moon made the place weird, like a dream. I opened the window a little, cool air chilled my forehead.

'Smooth...', Marley said, running his hand along the walnut veneer fascia. 'Becky this smooth?'

'Fuck you.'

'What? She shave, no?'

'Piss off.'

'Still with that Peter French dick, is she?'

'As far as I know.'

'Must be love. Bad form though, that time in first year. Jumping ship on ya just cause your ol' lad got canned.'

74

'I'd break off with him if I could.'

'Still go up there to see him every week?'

I nodded.

'When's he getting out?'

'Years.'

'Rough. He never told them where the few quid was put?'

'Don't think so. I wasn't at the court.'

'Did he—'

'No, he didn't tell me where he put it.'

'Alright, scan. Only askin'. You could be sleeping on it, Tommy.' Marley opened and closed the glove compartment. 'All that dough. It might be in your mattress! Never looked around for it?'

'I don't need it.'

'Not with this game! Maybe he gave it to your uncle?'

'Maybe.'

'Bad shit though, Tommy. Some bastard setting up your ol' lad like that. Never got the fella's name, no?'

'Underage witness. He's protected.'

'Wankers. It's some maze a shite, the law. I see it with the ol' lad every week— ah fuck!'

The blue sign, luminous jackets, torches flashing, came into view just beyond an overpass. It was too late to veer off.

'Let me out!' Marley grabbed the door handle, but the car automatically central locked during motion.

'What's wrong with ya?'

'Let's ditch it to fuck!'

'Jesus, do you want them on to us? Relax, you dickhead. Give me the permit. And put on your belt.' Marley dug into his jacket, he took out a green card and handed it to me, his hand shaking. A Fiat was parked on the hard shoulder. One guard spoke to the driver, the other was at the centre of the road, waving us on, looking back at the Fiat.

'She's telling you to keep going, thank fuck. They're busy with that Fiat.'

'She?' But the garda changed her signal at the last minute to a flat outstretched palm as we reached her. She waved for me to pull in behind the Fiat.

'Ah bollocks, she's pulling you over.'

The garda came across the front of the car, flashed her torch at the tax and insurance discs. Everything was in order, it was the first check we did. As she came around, I lowered the window.

'Hee-lo Constabulary,' I said, tongue pushed between my teeth.

'Good evening. Licence please.' I handed her the green card. Her eyes narrowed. 'What is this?'

'Is licence.' I smiled all the time, nodding my head, a technique to get people to believe you. I'd read about it on *StumbleUpon*. 'Of my country.'

The garda shone the torch on the card. 'Rory?'

'Yury, please.'

'You are Russian? What is your business here?'

'Holidays, please.' The ban garda pointed the torch at me. I guessed she was wondering about the lack of stubble around my jaw. She looked at the car, a 151 Mercedes CLS 300.

The garda squinted again at the card. I could barely pronounce the name printed. The only thing familiar was the greyscale photo, photoshopped before I'd sent it off to age me a few years. The licence had cost €400 online. Along with the key code scanner, and the dummy transponder key, Marley reckoned he had invested over a grand in our business of luxury car 're-appropriation', as he called it. There was a noise from the Fiat, the driver was shouting, waving his hands. I saw the other guard reach for his handcuffs.

'Fiona!'

The garda looked back. 'Drive safe.' She handed me the card.

'Tank you much.'

I drove slowly away. 'What about that, Jakey boy! Cool as fuck, hah?' I turned to Marley. I wanted to ruffle his hair or something. It was electric. I was buzzing. But he was watching the wing mirror.

'Stop jerking around, she'll see ya. Just as well she didn't run the loaded plates.'

'Worried about Pulse now, are ya? "Father sell oil." How did ya like that? Imagine if she'd spoke Russian?' I wanted to keep talking, it was like I couldn't say everything quick enough. 'How many cops speak Russian though in fairness? Maybe I'll say I'm from Belarus next time. Don't think they speak Russian there, do they? So much for Saturday nights, no checkpoints, clever bird.'

Marley looked out the window at the endless steel railing along the hard shoulder.

'The Oligarch son is fair convincing though, huh? Worked like a dream there.'

Marley lit a cigarette. 'Let's face it, Tommy, if that scan in the Fiat hadn't been goin' bananas that could have gone arseways—'

'What are you always saying? Chillax!'

We kept out of the city centre and off the ring roads and toll booths. I took a side street toward the industrial areas, into estates of towering warehouses, some with huge lettering along the roof, down networks of generic grey mazes, past steel chimneys and massive yards of containers, scrap metal, commercial vehicles. We came out onto a two-lane road that ran for miles north, along the coast. There were detached houses on the left, the calm sea on the right. The houses had window boxes, neat lawns and mostly mid-range 10 or 11 cars. The taste of salt came through. The streetlights drowned out the moon's rays, although we could see a silver track along the water which followed us all the way.

After about half an hour, we arrived at The Marina. It was a long pier. There were some large houses across from the water, mostly they were hidden with thick woods, electric gates, winding drives. You could see the multi-level roofs and balconies on some of them. Along the pier there were lots of yachts. Some were lit up. There were people on deck. I saw musicians, people in suits and flowing dresses drinking wine and cocktails. Down at the end of the pier there was a line of warehouse units, which the yacht owners could rent to store tools or whatever on shore.

Eric stood at the door of one of the units. He looked up under a thick mop of ginger hair, took out a remote, the roller door behind him rose, but he left the light inside off. I drove in. Eric followed me, the roller door came down. He turned on the lights, they were blinding for a second. The shed was large, a few units had been knocked in together, the place was all whitewashed walls, the floor polished concrete. It was jammed with new cars, none of which had plates: BMWs, Mercs, Lexus. There was a Range Rover in the corner. I parked up our Merc.

'Alrigh' lads,' Eric said as he looked around the car. 'Disabled the GPS, yeah?'

'Course,' I said. Eric went into a small portakabin at the wall. After a moment, he came out with an envelope and gave it to Marley. Then he led us out through a side door. We got into an 07 Toyota hatchback. He drove around the line of warehouses and along by the water's edge.

'What's going on in there,' I said from the back, as we passed the yachts.

'Boat parties. That's where the real brass is. Bankers, developers. Few politicians probably.' Eric stopped near the end of the yachts at a really big one. It was in darkness, we could mostly only see the shape. 'See that?' Eric's lights lit up the side. The yacht was labelled 'Sunseeker 115'. 'Worth about twenty million.'

'Did you say million?' I said.

'It's like a luxury house on a boat. Fella that owns it lives in Monaco. Inherited all his dough. Doesn't know what to do with it. He hasn't been out here in a couple of years. That's the sort of work yiz should get into. Bring that to Calais, I could get yiz half a mill.'

'Probably crazy security on it,' Marley said.

'It's all done online with them yokes now. And if you don't renew it, you're left out in the open. He hasn't renewed his.'

'How do you know that?' I said.

'No flashing green inside. That's the alarms. He hasn't bothered. Yachts are hardly ever stolen. Still, it's big money.'

'They're a bit harder than a car to drive,' I said.

'It's all done by computers. Google it. Worth the effort, I'd say.'

'Let's go, we'll miss the night bus,' Marley said, lighting up.

'How come you don't do it yourself?' I said.

'What?'

'Take that yacht.'

'I know me job. Yiz get it there. I'll do the rest.' It was hard to know if Eric was being serious. He drove on, the glow and noise of the yacht parties behind us.

Something hit the Perspex and I woke up. I looked at the window. A large brown head stared at me. I was lying on the near sofa bed, still wearing my clothes. I was going to let Tuohy sort out his cattle this time. I left them chewing the DPC around the windows of the new house, went down the road and up the boreen. I climbed in through the hedge and went up the path.

'Jack! The cattle are in again! They're eating shit off our new house!' I looked back and saw the Fiesta parked in its usual spot. I pushed the door and went inside, came into a kind of hallway, with a big internal window across from the door. I went left to the end, turned right into the big kitchen. Clocks ticked somewhere, but I couldn't see them. I smelt socks. There was a Stanley range at the fireplace across from me, a long table to the left at the back window. A Sacred Heart hung over the mantelpiece. To the right of the range, a press built into an alcove ran up to the timbered ceiling. Its narrow door was slightly open. All the shelves inside were lined with flattened newspaper. On the bottom, there were folded blankets, the type nobody used anymore because they were so itchy. Mam had them in our cottage. Further up, there were cardboard boxes, jugs, an oil lamp and at the top, a battered USA biscuit tin. Something caught my eye. I went over to the press, pulled the door back a little. I saw under the biscuit tin lid the corner of a fifty euro note. I stood back. There was an almost full bottle of Jameson on the window board of the internal window. Beside the window, there was another press with glass doors. There was a set of decorated plates tacked to the back behind the glass panels, cups and saucers along the front, thick with dust. We'd had something like that in the house at the end of the field. I found a small thick glass on a lower shelf beside a stack of plates.

'Jack? The cattle?' I half-filled the glass with whiskey. I took a good gulp. It was rotten, but then I got this blast of heat, first in my throat, then in my chest, stomach, arms, legs, down to my toes. I looked up at the biscuit tin. I finished off the glass, tried to find something to stand up on. I heard a wrapper behind me. I turned. Tuohy stood in a doorway in the far corner, in loose pyjamas. He put a chupa-chup in his mouth.

'The cattle, Jack,' I said, caring less about him. 'They need to be sorted out.' I heard a rough gear change. There was a car driving up The Mackon. I looked out the internal window, through the yellowed glass of Tuohy's front door. Something passed by. I could hear the Death Notices theme tune in the distance.

The light blue of Our Lady's shawl blurred into the grey of the sky behind. She tapped and rocked all the way from The Mackon. The radio presenter offered sympathies to the dead from all at the station. The segment finished up with the usual organ music. I was dying for a fag as we came near the avenue. 'Need to get a jambon in the shop.'

'Did you not bring a sandwich, Tommy? Didn't I leave stuff there for you yesterday? Ham and cheese and a loaf?' Ann said.

'Hadn't time to make it this morning.'

'Do you have money?'

'Yeah.'

'You're making it last well. Do you want another fiver?'

'No thanks.'

'Are you okay, your eyes look a bit bloodshot?'

'I've a lift to The Mackon with one of the lads this evening, Ann. You don't need to bother collecting me.'

'What about your dinner?'

'I'll get a pizza.'

'You're not going home early again, are you?' Ann looked at me as she puffed on her e-fag.

'I'll see ya later.' I shut the door before she could say anything else. I went around the short wall to the shop. Maurice was coming from the gas cylinders. He stood in between me and the entrance.

'Good morning, Tommy. How are you today?' He was beaming. His tie lifted in the breeze. 'Don't forget to check out our special filled doughnuts Marcel baked early this morning. I had one myself, it was absolutely gorgeous, real buttery chocolate sauce and cream in them.' A woman stopped between us.

'Maurice dear, how is poor Gerald?'

'Oh, the same, Mrs Kinneally.'

'It's awful. And your granny in St Michael's as well. How is she?'

'Oh, she's much the same too, Mrs Kinneally. But how are you, are you getting your veggies today? We have fresh carrots in there this morning…'. I stepped around them and went in to get my fags.

A headache came on as I smoked and walked up the avenue. I'd had enough of the day already and it was only half eight. Once McDermott came with the register, I could go, but I didn't know when that would be. That was probably why he never came at the same time. Two first years were dragged in the green door of the convent section by the latest crop of Leaving Certs as I went around by the poplar island. The Wet Room did good business in September, before the first years figured out the shortcuts to avoid attacks. I could still hear the squeals and howls as I

84

neared the entrance. Two more first years were at the doors, watching me. One said something to the other and he ran up, waving a fiver.

'Can we give it to you? You're with Mr Marley?' He held the note out.

'Marley not in today?'

'No.'

While Marley had been at less than half of the classes in second year, he'd still been in a lot more than me. He had gotten into the 'Student Protection League', organised by some fourth years. Their main activity was getting 'donations' from new students. Marley had learned fast and already the first years were queueing up to pay him.

'I don't want your money.' The first year stared at me as I passed.

By lunch, there was still no sign of the V.P. I had a smoke in the woods. It wasn't the same without Marley and his antics. Lally and the other square heads were just too boring. I went inside and played cards in the Assembly Hall with a few fourth years. Rebecca and Peter French sat in the stairwell under the balcony. Through the table tennis games going on, I could only see their shapes in the dark shadows, but I guessed they were shifting and maybe even doing a bit of pawing. At two o'clock I couldn't face going down into the French class. I'd given up the last of the honours courses in the summer term and now took pass in everything. It was easy to dream at the back of ordinary level, even though Mr Coyne prodded me now and again with questions about perspective and the 'artistic process'. Sherlock's parking space was empty at the front doors, he was still gone to dinner. I hurried out the avenue. It would be just one more absence.

There was no traffic and I had to walk all the way out to The Mackon. At the mobile, there were visitors. Midnight's jeep and another car were parked outside. I had to check to make sure I wasn't seeing things. It really was Pock's Audi. Midnight had told me that Pock went abroad when dad got arrested, even though dad hadn't told the guards anything. The young squealer they'd got into court had done just enough talking to get dad put away.

They had turned everything upside-down. I decided it was better not to show my face. They'd come when they'd thought I wouldn't be around for some reason and it was hard to know how they'd react if I arrived in the middle of whatever it was they were doing. I edged around by the fence to the site behind. I crept in the back door of the new house. At the half-built sitting room window, I looked in over the sill. They were tidying up. They dropped dad's mattress into place, even making the bed as it had been. Pots and pans were shoved into presses. I could only hear muffled voices. I knew they'd go before four o'clock. I didn't dare smoke, sat into the fireplace and took out my phone, hooked onto our internet. I googled 'Sunseeker 115'.

Stealing a yacht like that wasn't an option. You needed a crew of experts to operate it. Some of the models sold for forty and fifty million, they were like penthouse suites that floated. Theft was rare and complex but could be highly profitable. Maybe it was a future career. For now, online motor ads were my level. I looked up luxury cars for sale in the area, the type suitable for me and Marley to come and 'move on'.

The visitors left about half three. Inside, everything seemed exactly as I'd left it, down to the way my clothes had been tossed on dad's bed. Army discipline. They'd most likely taken photos before they started. I took out a tin of beans, grilled some bread, made scrambled eggs in the pan. I poured a glass of water and sat at the table. As I ate, my eyes traced the outline of the far sofa bed, under the table, the cavity behind the cooker, dad's double bed and mam's old medicine books, down along the shower and toilet.

When I'd eaten, I sat back, lit a fag. Through the furls of smoke, something glinted over the cooker. I got up, went to the press. The key and a keyring in the shape of the Defence Forces logo hung from the lock. Midnight had left it after him. Army discipline. Maybe that was why Midnight had never made it past the rank of Private.

The unit had been locked since dad left it. He must have given Midnight the key. I opened it up. Inside there was a steel flask, a bunch of maps, an elaborate but well-rusted utility penknife, a few rolls of fishing line, reels, flies, hooks and, slid in at the side, two very dusty bottles of Hennessy Cognac. At the back, I saw the rifle in parts, amongst a can of gun oil and a cardboard box of rounds. The gun had been a 30th birthday present for dad. Midnight had used some of his military contacts to get it, around the time mam went away. But I'd never seen dad use it, except the time he'd shot Ash in the head.

I pulled out the barrel with the other parts and brought everything over to the table. I took out one of the bottles of brandy, wiped the dust off the cap and opened it. It smelt like varnish. I half-filled a mug, downed a good gulp. Another belt of heat.

I opened the laptop and googled 'Remington L15 VTR Tactical', which was inscribed on the barrel. It was an older model, but still popular with some game hunters. I downloaded a PDF of the owner's manual. I followed the instructions to assemble the weapon. It took a while as I sipped brandy after each step. I locked the breech block into the butt, slid in the loading bolt and spring, the firing pin, clicked on the breech casing over the top, fitted the telescopic sights. I got out the rounds. You had to push them into the spring-loaded magazine. I clicked the mag. onto the base of the breech.

When I had the gun assembled, I pulled back the bolt and clicked it. This shoved a round up the breech. I finished off the mug of brandy as I read the PDF, the words doubling. There were three modes of operation: 'S' was the safety catch, the gun wouldn't fire. 'R' was for repetition, the gun would expel one round at a time. 'A' stood for automatic. That setting allowed rapid discharge of the magazine.

I aimed at the ceiling, changed the lever for 'A' to 'S'. I got a semi as I turned the gun, fitted my lips around the barrel. My finger was on the trigger. One squeeze and everything would be over.

A car stopped outside. Through the Perspex, I saw a Nissan, two-door hatchback. I slid the rifle and rounds under the sofa bed, put the brandy in the press. I locked it and put the key in my pocket. A woman got out of the car.

She looked older, maybe thirties. She wore a grey suit and carried a laptop case.

'Hello!' she smiled, as I opened the door. She had real white teeth. I liked her perfume.

'Tommy, is it? I'm Margaret O'Dea, from social services. I'm your appointed Juvenile Liaison Officer. Great to finally meet you!' She pulled an ID card from a little pouch on the front of the case and showed it to me. She looked much younger in her photo. I stood back and Margaret O'Dea came into the mobile.

Margaret O'Dea moved her thick heeled shoes around on the patch of worn carpet under the table, like there wasn't enough room for her. She had the laptop case open. She slid out a MacBook, a foolscap pad, a few pens and some forms. There was a smell of paper and glue. I heard the Apple start-up tone. I saw her looking over at the cooking area. In the sink, a plate stood upended in a small pool of brown water, a patch of gravy skim across it. On the draining board, me and Marley's Sunday night pizza boxes were tossed, beside a fork stuck to a hardened twirl of pasta. Beyond, on dad's bed, there were some busted snack boxes. A rubbish bag was underneath on the floor, a milk carton sticking out the top. There were t-shirts and socks everywhere. I only saw these things when there was someone else in the mobile.

'First of all, Tommy, I want to apologise to you.' Margaret O'Dea smiled faintly. 'I told your uncle when I met him on Friday, but I wanted to reiterate it here. As I'm sure you know, there was a change of administration around the time your dad went away, an unfortunate coincidence, and a lot of middle management was rotated.

The upshot of this was that your file went into the system at a time of reorganisation and I'm afraid it wasn't attended to until now.' Margaret O'Dea clicked the keyboard. 'I'm really sorry about that, Tommy.'

'Do you want a cup of tea?'

'No thank you, good lad, you're very sweet, but I don't drink tea. I'm just here today for a preliminary meeting with yourself, to ask a few questions about your living arrangements. Jeremy signed off on it on Friday. He is actually your legal guardian at present, did you know that?'

'No.'

'Don't worry, this is not an exam or anything like that.' She was smiling again. 'Just a few questions, there are no wrong answers. It's really to make absolutely certain that you are getting all the support you need at this important time in your life, Tommy. You are fifteen...'. She glanced at the MacBook, clicked the screen. 'Sixteen in a few months.' I felt like a cigarette but decided against it. She wrote something on the foolscap, drew a line across. 'To start with, your uncle stays here with you now, isn't that right?'

'Sometimes I stay with him.'

'He was in the army?'

'Yeah, he did a few tours of Lebanon.'

'And tell me Tommy, after your father went to prison, why didn't you move in to your uncle's house in Cloonloch?'

'It's only a one-bed he had. He said there'd be some hassle with the council.'

'Right.' She nodded, writing. 'I see you're a fan of fast food. That's not all you eat, is it?'

'I have other stuff as well…'. I thought for a few seconds. 'Rashers and eggs and …potatoes.'

'Do you cook? Or does Jeremy do that for you?' I laughed. The idea of Midnight with a frying pan was too funny.

'Ann does the cooking mostly.'

'Now, who is Ann?'

'Ann is…Midnight's girlfriend. Jeremy's girlfriend.'

'I see. How often does Ann cook for you?'

'She was here on Friday…'. I was getting tired of the questions.

'A few times a week, is it?'

'Maybe. Yeah.' She wrote all of this down.

'And does Ann do your washing too?'

'Sometimes…other times she reckons the pots need steeping and tells me to do them after she's gone.'

'I see.' Margaret O'Dea nodded toward the crowded sink. 'But what I meant by washing was your laundry. I don't see a washing machine.'

'Ann takes a bag…every week, I think. Brings back the washed stuff.'

'Fair play to Ann, eh?' She wrote 'Ann' down in big letters on the page. 'But you have lots of homework to be getting on with, don't you, Tommy? Junior Cert this year, isn't it?'

Margaret O'Dea wanted to know how often I visited mam and dad, if I showered every day, how much time I spent on homework, how much time out at the weekend, where I went and how I got there and a million other nonsense things. I told her any old rubbish after a while. I left out my activities with Marley. An hour or so later, she had pages filled, she was shaking her wrist.

'Sure you don't want a coffee?'

'I don't drink caffeine at all, Tommy. I'll have a glass of water, if you have some there.' I filled her a glass from the five-gallon drum, she took a good gulp. 'Now, I have to go back to the office and type all this up. I have your phone number, so I'll be in touch again in a few days. We might have another chat about things then, is that okay?' She smiled. 'As I was saying, the social services where I work are responsible for making sure youths like yourself aren't neglected in a social, emotional or educational sense, just because both parents can't be present for whatever reason. You see Tommy, it's very important that all young people are given every chance to achieve their full potential. Sometimes external circumstances, none of which are the youth's fault can get in the way and it's our job to offer you help, advice and support and, in some circumstances, intervene when necessary during this period.'

I looked up across the table. 'Why? What's going to happen?'

'Sorry?'

'You said intervene?'

'Your case will be assessed by my board now that you've given me a fuller picture. I'll get back to you within a couple of days.' She was getting up, shaking my hand. The questions were over, and now she couldn't get out of there quick enough. It felt like I'd been at confessions and

I'd made some complaint about mam and dad or Midnight and Ann.

We went up the avenue of Greenwood Prison in Midnight's jeep, past big black gates that looked like they hadn't been closed for years and lines of pine trees either side, small signs of '5' for the speed limit. At the top, there was a grass roundabout in front of the entrance. The building had been converted into a jail in the 1980s from a derelict mental hospital. Along with decorative corner stones and plain reveals, the original white pebble-dashed building still had rusty metal bars on all the windows. Most of the old section was now offices, the prisoners were housed in a group of newer grey buildings out the back. The complex was in the middle of a copse wood, miles from anywhere. Perfect for medium to long-term prisoners, not ideal for visitors. There were no buses or trains. Midnight had to drive me out there every Tuesday evening. We had to go through three checkpoints every time, one where we gave ours and dad's name, another where you handed in the items you were bringing which were put in a tray, a third where you went through a laser beam in a special doorway. The visitors' room was crowded, one guard stood at the door, scrolling on his phone. We found dad near a window. The tray had got there before us and he was leafing through the local paper. 'That young fella has another big ad. out this week.'

'Who?'

'Young O'Malley.'

'He's making a good job of the place since the ol' fella had the stroke,' Midnight said, as he pulled out the other chair. I stood awkwardly at the table. 'Lovely cream doughnuts in there now. I had a couple the last day I brought Tommy in to school.'

'He'll run it into the ground same as the ol' fella. How are you, lad?'

'Alright.'

'He had a visitor.'

'Who?' Dad folded up the paper.

'Social worker,' I said.

'What did she want?'

'Rake of questions. About living alone, stuff like that.'

'But you're not living alone. Isn't Midnight and Ann looking after you?'

'That's what I told her.'

'Good lad, good lad. Ye are bringing him to school and all that?'

'Course we are, Joe.'

'Good. Fucking nosy cunt. Tell her you don't need any poxy help next time she comes. Hey Mid, I heard in here the last day that little bastard squealer is flat out up the country, shifting hot high-end wagons. Did you hear that?'

Midnight coughed deeply, his phlegm bubbling in his throat. After he'd snorted something into a ball of tissue paper he'd pulled from an inside pocket, he said 'No, no. I didn't hear any of that. I thought he was lying low?'

'The neck on him. No word of the other lad?'

'You mean Pock?'

'No, I mean Pope John Paul the second.'

'Not a thing.'

'Still abroad, is he?'

'Suppose he must be. I haven't been talking to him.'

'Jesus Christ, what's this about?' Dad had one of the letters open. I felt hot as I saw Sherlock's signature at the bottom.

'I thought you said ye were bringing him to school?'

'We are, we are, every morning either meself or Ann bring him in—'

'Then why is this Sherlock going on about him being only at school a couple of days since the new year started? "Last year's performance cannot be repeated," he says. He wants to meet you and sort it out.'

Midnight turned to me.

'Are you not going in after us bringing you all the way to the gates?'

'Yeah I am.'

'He must be mitching before the registration Joe, that's all I can say.'

'I'm not mitching.'

'Where the hell are ya then, for the love of God!'

'Fuck's sake!' Dad banged the table with his fist. The prison guard looked up, casually slid the phone into his pocket, came over.

'Everything alright, Joe?'

'This fella won't go in to school.'

'Ah, the youth!' the guard said, shaking his head as he returned to his post.

'You better go in and see him.'

'I will, I will. Shylock, is it?'

'Sherlock.'

'The hearing is gone to pot, the bombs out in The Leb, you see—'

'And you,' dad turned to me, glaring. 'If you don't go to school, how are you going to learn anything? Do you want to be arsin' about like me and him for the rest of your days?'

'I served my country,' Midnight said.

'Until you decided it should start serving you. Some of us worked that out a bit quicker, Uncle Jeremy!'

As they went on, I looked beyond dad, through the glass laced with high tensile steel, I could see the thin top branches of the copse, lifting in the wind. I wondered then what it'd be like to live there like the birds, in a nest high up, surrounded by the green of leaves.

Midnight dropped me off at eight. I was starving again and heated up another Dr Oetker. While I was waiting, I went on Done Deal. I found a Mercedes XLS 300 for sale in Cloonloch. Three years old, €17,500 o.n.o. But with Marley's device, it'd come for free. I texted him the link to the site. After, I went out to Ash's grave, pulled a few weeds from around the stones. I went up through The Mackon as the light faded away, to the other side of the village, where the scraggy ground gave way to the bog that surrounded our village. I walked past the tracks where turf had been tossed out by a hopper, turned, footed into little pyramids, bagged and taken away, then unloaded and rooked up in barns around The Mackon. Dad had saved turf out here a few times. I remembered going out with him when I was six or seven, before we moved from mam's cottage to the mobile. The last of the year's cut was scattered on the side of the road.

I climbed over a fence. I walked across the bog land for miles. The ground improved a bit, more grassy and stony as I passed by the school and Ballincalty. Eventually, I came to the boreen which led up to The Castle. The ground got marshy again. I went through the gate, up past the old shell. I climbed a fence behind the barns. I walked along the narrow dirt track and came to the swamp where they'd dumped all the scrap. Some wires, electrical stuff that hadn't sunk, were stuck to a bunch of reeds. There'd been a lot of rain over the past weeks, the boggy muck goo was diluted, it was overflowing at the back into a forestry managed block of pine trees. I tramped into the swamp, over thin brown clumps of bog grass, the ground springy underneath. Water began to seep into my runners. Dad once said it was thirty-foot deep in parts. I stopped, feeling the cold wet. Birds chirped somewhere. I remembered something the geography teacher had said the week before, her voice was squeaky and loud, I couldn't daydream. Birds came down here from the Antarctic in the winter months. For them our climate was real mild. It was the northern birds that sang around me.

With the water thinning it out, the top of the swamp was pure flat in places, it reminded me of tin foil. I saw mam rolling up sandwiches for my day in Junior Infants down in The Mackon village school. I lifted my leg to step forward. The water came up past my ankles, the movement sent a ripple drifting out towards the centre. I watched as it slowed and then faded, melting into the perfect surface.

At first break, I watched the two detectives from the ATM raid leave Sherlock's office. They both shook hands with the Principal. Outside, I leaned against an Assembly Hall windowsill, looking across through the glass, along the hall, a fag hooked in my fingers. It had been a slow morning. I'd sat at the back of French, English and Business Studies, dreaming as I stared out the windows. No sign of McDermott and unofficial permission to go home. There was still no Marley since the weekend. He wasn't answering any of my texts or Facebook messages. Another bunch of worried first years had hassled me about who they should be giving their 'donations' to. I scrolled down and sent him another poke. I wanted to plan the Friday night operation.

The V.P. came during the first class of double Science. Straight after, I skipped out on an emergency toilet break. The school was calm, this was my favourite time to wander the halls. All I could hear was the low drone of teachers behind closed doors, a hum of a heating fan somewhere in the ceilings. I sat in the cubicle on the toilet lid, hands together. The door in front of me was scribbled all over in black and blue marker: 'Meet here 9 on Mondays for a good time', 'Willie Downes sucks cock'. There were drawings of dicks, tits, swastikas, machine guns of varying skill. I wondered what the girls drew on their doors.

I put my head down between my legs. The bell rang. Noises came then, tables, chairs dragging, sneakers padding the rubber floor covering. My class would be moving on to History. My schoolbag was left at my stool in the Lab., across from Rebecca and Peter French, but I didn't much care. I'd already been marked present. I decided I'd just walk home. I rang Midnight. For once, he answered the phone.

'Yeah?' There was a bout of coughing.

'You don't need to come this evening. I've a lift.'

'Are ya sure?' Midnight managed eventually. 'We're going to the Home later. I'll be there at six so. Ann is coming to do a bit of tidy-up she says…'. He was still coughing as I hung up. I went down through the Resource Area, some of my class were already on the way to the History room. Out of the corner of my eye, I saw Rebecca and Peter French hold hands.

The late morning lull had hit the town. Maurice was in the forecourt, filling petrol for someone, he smiled at me as I passed. I went across the road and into The Olde Tree. The place was empty. Sky News was on low behind the counter. I could smell porter, lemon floor cleaner in the toilets. I sat at the end of the bar, fidgeted with a beermat. It was getting on for noon. There were noises in the pot room. Jimmy came out with his son, their backs to me.

'Now take your time and you'll be grand. Listen to the orders and get them to repeat them if you have to. Check the change twice before you give it out, alright? The barrels are all full or near it, so you should be fine. Give me a bell if you've any problems. Good man.' Jimmy went out the back. The son picked up a cloth and then saw me. He came down to the end of the counter.

'Pint of Guinness,' I said, taking out a fiver. The son looked at me, grey trousers, stained runners, plastic jacket hiding my school crested jumper. He looked around the bar quickly. He shrugged, pulled the pint.

The stout tasted rotten, like all drink, but you didn't buy it for the flavour. On the TV, there was a continuous buzz of presenters and reporters exchanging words, show jingles, adverts. Jimmy's son sat on the stool behind the counter, foam sticking out from the leather covering. He watched the TV, slowly tearing pieces off a beermat and flicking them to the floor. He picked up his phone every few seconds, scrolled it, then tossed it back to the drip trays at the beer taps. When I'd the pint nearly finished, I played a few games of pool on my own, smoked a fag in the back-garden gazebo, had a few goes on the fruit machine, soon I was broke.

I went back out into the street, the light blinded me. I went across toward O'Malley's and then to the house beside it. It was a two-storey detached. Black wrought iron gates hung on moulded pillars. They led into a tarmacked drive. The lawn to the right was neatly mown, bordered by a trimmed two-foot high box hedge. A stone path ran down the middle, around a polished concrete fountain, where water spilled out of a fish's mouth, dripping into a green-tinted pool below. I went up the drive, around the side of the house, to the back garden, passing pruned pink rosebushes, a coiled mustard water hose, a golden varnished bird feeder.

There was a patio area in front of glass double doors, a wooden table and chairs under a large green umbrella. I looked in through the reflecting windows. I could see the walnut kitchen, granite worktops, marbled floor, red and white splashback tiles.

Marley sat in his boxers at the island in the centre, wearing huge Sony headphones. He stared at the laptop screen. Two naked women rubbed suds on each other in an enormous bathtub. Marley took up a piece of toast.

I thought I should knock on the glass, tell him it was alright for some bastards, sitting at home, wanking half the day while others had to wait around for that red-bearded fool of a vice-principal and his roll book and that it was all a load of bollocks. We'd have tea and toast, and we could slag off Sherlock, have a few fags, then we could plan that operation on Friday night.

Marley clicked the keyboard, the naked women vanished, the school website appeared. He opened 'First Year' and then a PDF. It was something about 20th-century history. He chewed as he read.

Nora pulled my arm as I passed her. Her eyes were wide, she was smiling. Her grip on my jacket was tight. There was a smell of damp newspapers off her. 'Gerald? Gerald? It's me?'

'I'm…not your son.'

'Oh.' She let go and sat down. 'I'm going home this evening, you see.'

My mother sat by the window. She looked up as we came to the bed, her eyes unusually bright.

'Tommy! Give your mother a kiss!' First I thought it was a tape recording. She hadn't called me by name in years. I kissed her on the cheek. 'How are you, my boy?'

'Fine.'

'The uniform suits you so well.' I was excited, it looked like we might even have a conversation. She gazed then across to the other window bed, where there was only a mattress. Mam stared for a long time. The conversation was over.

'It's these new tablets they have her on,' Midnight said. 'They seem to be helping her a bit. It's all a money racket if you ask me. Them drug companies. Releasing cures when it suits them. Never trust money men, that's what I say. It's all fixed.'

'How are you today, Shelia?' It was the duty nurse, she came to the end of mam's bed, looked through the file. 'Are you her son?' The nurse smiled at me. 'Good lad. Does her the power of good to have visitors.'

'We do the best we can,' Midnight said.

'Pat! Pat!' Mam's eyes opened wide, she shivered as though an electrical charge ran through her. I closed my eyes.

I could hear hot oil spitting in the mobile as we got out of the jeep. Inside, Ann wore an apron of red cherries, her hair was tied back, steam patched the lens of her glasses, she shook the pan around on the blue gas flame, the yellow and white of the eggs bubbled and spat. The mobile was hoovered and polished, everywhere smelt nice. 'Are you okay, Tommy?' Ann said as we came in. 'How is your poor mother?'

'On new tablets,' Midnight said, sitting on the far sofa bed. He lay back, put his sand boots up. 'It's an awful sight, her zonin' in and out of it. She was better off the other way, I think meself.'

'Get your feet off them cushions! Jeremy! Do you hear me?' Ann took up the sweeping brush, went toward my uncle. 'I just cleaned them with Febreze!'

'Ah, for the love of God, woman!' Midnight sat up, eyeing the brush. He pulled out his cigars as Ann returned to the frying pan.

'And don't light up one of them dirty rotten things after me just spraying the place with air freshener for the young lad!'

'Ah, Jesus!' Midnight put away the yellow box. 'Give us one of your fags, so.'

'Can't you wait until after your tea now? Anyway, I don't have any. I don't use tobacco anymore. I just take the electronic cigarette.'

'Electronic cigarettes!' Midnight snorted. 'What's the world comin' to, even the smoke has gone plastic!' I had my phone out, scrolled down through Facebook.

'Do you want some fried bread with this, Tommy?' Ann said, trimming the ends of the eggs.

'Okay.'

'How did you get on with your dad yesterday?'

'Fine.'

'God help him, stuck in there, day in and day out.' Ann pressed a slice of bread onto the pan.

'He's pool champ of the block, anyhow,' Midnight said, fumbling around in his jacket, before pulling out a can of Dutch Gold. 'He went mad over that letter, though.'

'What letter?' Ann said.

Midnight opened the can, sipped. 'From Sheridan, the principal of the school.'

'It's Sherlock.' I said.

'I'm surprised you know, the amount of time you're there!'

Rebecca and Peter French had set up a Facebook page called 'Becky and Pete'. There were loads of photos of them together in different places over the summer. They'd just jointly posted something about the basement disco in the Cloonloch Arms Hotel on Friday night, a start of the year thing, most of Junior Cert was going. It reminded me of the job with the CLS 300. I went on to the motor ad. site. The car still hadn't been sold. I saved the mobile number.

'What was the letter about?' Ann said, fish slicing the eggs and bread onto plates, pouring out tea.

'Tommy not going in to school half the time. Yer man wants to see me tomorrow morning.'

'Ah Tommy, what's this about? Aren't we bringing you in every day?' She brought over two plates of eggs and bread.

'It's a mix up with the register,' I said. I looked up from the phone, saw Midnight winking at Ann and shaking his head, the greying curls losing specks of dandruff on the table. 'No, it is. We have a lot of free classes and I do miss the roll call. It happens a lot of people.'

'You must be missing a lot to be getting letters from the Principal, Tommy,' Ann said.

'Ah, the youth,' Midnight said, dipping his bread in egg yolk. 'If you saw the things I saw in Leb, you'd go to school, I tell ya.'

'Staying here on your own every night, all the same.' Ann wiped the counter with a dishcloth. 'It's not good for a schoolboy. Maybe you could stay with Jeremy in the box room the odd night for the winter.' Midnight coughed.

'If the council hear about that—'

'Ah, be quiet. How long am I staying there with you and my little car parked outside and we had no trouble. If it's only an odd time, they don't care. What do you think, Tommy? Do you want to come over tonight? Jeremy could bring you straight to Ballincalty tomorrow if you bring your schoolbag with you?'

'Nah, I'm fine here.'

'Now, Tommy—,' Ann stared at me.

'Alright, alright.' I didn't want to argue with someone who made such a tasty tea of eggs and fried bread.

Midnight's house was in a council estate on the outskirts of Cloonloch. It was a one-bedroom place, with a tiny box room at the front beside the entrance door where he put ex-military callers up for the night, a bathroom to the right and a kitchen sitter at the back. Ann got me set up in the box room on Midnight's army camp bed and sleeping bag, some of the many things my uncle had taken as unofficial retirement presents by 'special arrangement' with his drinking partner, the quartermaster.

'Do you want a cup of tea?' Ann said as I sat on the small couch in the sitting area.

'Be sure to put at least eight tea bags in the pot,' Midnight shouted, midstream in the toilet.

'Do you want to be able to stand on it? Sit there, Tommy, good lad. I have some lovely éclairs in the fridge. I got them today fresh from Rourke's.' Midnight sat beside me, lit a King Edward with his zippo.

'Fresh enough in here and all.' Midnight shivered. 'Is the oil gone again?'

'Did you get some?' Ann said, arranging an éclair on a small plate at the worktop.

'I'm a bit strapped until the 25th, that's the problem.'

'The 25th, the 25th. That's the same old tune every month.' Ann put the éclair and a mug of steaming tea in front of me on a small wooden table. She sat across in an armchair, opened her handbag. 'Now, it is cold alright. Do you feel it, Tommy?'

'A bit.'

'Poor lad.' Ann took a twenty out and put it on the table.

'Ah, will you not go down and get it?' my uncle said, looking at it.

'Is it not enough I'm buying it? I suppose you would have an old woman lugging around a big can of oil, alright.' Midnight sat back, puffing on the cigar.

'Put the telly on there lad, till we see what canter is on.' I turned on the telly, found Channel 4 racing. The commentator's tone was relaxed, he outlined the going, the jockeys, each horse's recent form. Midnight was already sitting up, tapping his knees as he always did at the sight of the colourful jockeys and the flashing feed of odds on a screen. It was the only time I ever saw him excited. The cream in the bun was real fresh, the tea milky and sweet. I felt warm sitting there, much better than back in the mobile, although I wasn't sure why. Midnight shivered again. He turned to Ann.

'Will you get the oil, if I go I'll miss the race?'

'You can watch it in the fresh air, so.' Ann filled the cartridge of her e-fag.

'For the love of God!' Midnight grabbed the twenty. 'Come on Tommy. Swallow that beast, you may as well come for the spin.'

We drove out of Midnight's estate in the jeep, back through the streets of Cloonloch. He passed the service station that sold five-gallon drums of heating oil. On the main street, he stopped outside Ladbrokes. He hurried inside, as quick as his triangular shape would allow.

'Who's racing?' I said, when he came back out a few minutes later, his thick fingers around a yellow slip.

'The Fairyhouse handicap. A fella in there knows
the trainer. Bold Boy at twenty to
one. It's all set up with the other jockeys.'

'No way. They say that, but it's not really fixed.'

'Ah, the youth. Everything is fixed, lad.' Midnight turned at the top of the street. He passed the service station again on the way out.

'What about the oil?'

Midnight drove into another estate, this one had a high wall around it, tall pillars at the entrance. All the houses were detached, they had bay windows and tarmacked drives. There were flower boxes on the windowsills, and the curtains were tied back behind the blinds. 151, 152 jeeps and cars were parked at the front doors. None were very lit up, mostly there was just a sitting room or hall light and front door side lamps. One was in complete darkness, there were no cars outside. Here Midnight turned in, stopped right outside the front door.

'Who lives here?'

'Come on.'

We got out. The estate was real quiet. I looked across the common ground, neatly mown, to the bay window in the house the other side. Inside there was a big screen TV in the corner, a large white marble fireplace, fire burning. I could see a pair of socked feet out on a cream leather sofa. A small boy ran across the room waving a toy.

Midnight opened the back of the jeep. He pulled out an empty five-gallon drum and an adjustable spanner. He handed me the drum and led me around the side of the house. He opened a wooden gate, and we came into the back garden. There was a stone patio, a pair of swings on a bright green steel tripod, a garden shed in the corner. The dark shape of an oil tank seemed to float beside the shed, the three block pillars underneath hidden in the shadows. Midnight went straight to the tank, twisting the nut on the oil line with the spanner. 'What if somebody comes?' I whispered, looking out at the drive. 'Your jeep will be boxed in.'

'Did you say your prayers this morning, lad?'

111

'Wouldn't it be better to park out on the street?'

'Do you want to be hauling a full drum all the way out there, with security cams and toddlers with flip pads or whatever they're called tapin' the whole thing?'

'Yeah, but–'

'If they block us, we'll say we work for the council and have to go urgent. They'll be too spooked to say anything if we keep going. We'll tell them there's…there's a water leak at the hospital.'

'What hospital?'

'Ah! You think too much, lad! Come over here with the drum, for the love of God, and stop asking questions. Come on, look lively!' I took the lid off the drum, held it under the pipe. When Midnight twisted the nut all the way, he pushed the sleeve back. The line came loose. A thick, steely smell rose as oil flowed into the drum. 'Aisy money,' Midnight said. I held the container steady as he wandered around the garden, looking in the windows of the house and shed, jerking the swing set, before pissing into the rosebushes.

Some oil spattered on my fingers, the handle of the drum got slippy. I lost concentration for a second, the drum slid out of my grip and fell to the path. It made a deep thump sound, turned on its side, oil flowed everywhere.

'Ya fuckin' eejit!' Midnight growled, zipping his fly up, hopping across. He smacked me on the head, picked the drum up and held it under the disconnected pipe. 'See that stain! Now the bitches will know I come.' His phone vibrated in his pocket. 'Hold this, that text must be the bookies.' He pulled out the phone. 'Ah, for the love of

God.' The screen lit up his face. 'Bold Boy. Not even placed.'

'I thought it was all fixed,' I said, the drum weighing me down again.

'It is. Just I'm not the one fixin' it.' When the drum was almost full, Midnight slid back the line into the sleeve, tightened the nut. I screwed on the lid, hauled the drum round to the back of the jeep. He had the motor running as I got in and we drove out of the estate in silence.

Dad had a red knitted cap on as he went out the back door. The white frost coated the stone walls in the fields outside. 'Pull it down over your ears, Joker, it's freezing today!' Mam smiled at the table. Dad looked in the window and pulled the wool down.

'What's that Shee, I can't hear ya!'

'Go on! And don't be late this evening, I'm making Shepherd's Pie!'

Mam buttered a piece of toast, dipped the knife in the pot of orange peel marmalade.

I couldn't breathe, I pulled the top of the army green sleeping bag down and stared out the little box room window to the yellow street light.

We stood at the radiator outside Sherlock's office. Students hurried to first classes, some of them staring at us. Ann searched in her beige handbag.

'Is he usually this late?' She dabbed her face with a folded cloth handkerchief. She was wearing some old type perfume. It reminded me of mam.

'Don't know. Never was waiting for him before.' Not true. Me and Marley had made many trips to the office in second year.

'Let's hope you don't make a habit of it. It's an awful thing to have someone from your family called in to the Principal's office, Tommy. I hope this will make you knuckle down a bit and get on with your work.' Ann meant well, but she could be awful annoying at times. Sherlock came around the corner. He stopped at Ann.

'Thank you for coming. Mrs O'Toole is it?'

'It's Miss. Miss Gillhooley.'

'Ah yes.' Sherlock shook Ann's hand weakly. He took a bunch of keys and opened the door. There was a carpet inside, wallpaper, a walnut desk, a soft office chair.

There were two hard seats in front. He waved us to sit. 'It's good to finally meet some of Tommy's family.'

'I'm not strictly related, Principal. I'm standing in. His uncle Jeremy would have come, but he has a bad back. It was playing up this morning. He was a soldier out in Lebanon.'

'I see.' Sherlock fidgeted with a pen. 'I wanted to talk to you today about Tommy's attendance record as a matter of urgency. As you'll know, Tommy is doing his Junior Cert next summer, and regular classes are essential for all the coursework. We are still in September and Tommy has already missed eleven days. It's not as though this is a new situation. He was absent for much of last year too. We never had sick notes or explanations of any kind. I sent several letters over there to The Mackon—,' Sherlock waved at the window, as though to some far-off land, 'But there was never any response, until I got by chance Mr Wall's home address in Cloonloch over the summer.'

Ann glared at me. 'Tommy! What's going on?' She looked at Sherlock. 'Every morning either me or Jeremy brings the lad in to the school gates, Principal. Sometimes we're not able to collect him, and he gets home with one of the other village kids. But we always bring him in for nine o'clock, Mr Sharlaton.'

'Yes. But I'm afraid he does not seem to be making it all the way up the avenue. Now, as I'm sure you'll appreciate, we have inspectors coming regularly ourselves. We cannot have registered students perennially absent.'

'I'm disappointed, Tommy,' Ann said. I didn't like it at all. It was as though I'd told a joke and no one laughed.

'Now what I want to establish today is exactly what Tommy wants from Ballincalty Secondary. Even when he does make it into class, he is not participating in any meaningful way. From what the teachers tell me, he is in a world of his own most of the time. Even in the Art Room, where he has shown some promise in the past.'

I'd never been sitting so close to the window in Sherlock's office, never sitting at all in there actually, and I couldn't believe the view he had from his desk. He overlooked the Resource Area roof, right across the tennis courts and straight down the paths of the smoking wood. It was no wonder he caught so many puffing.

He went on for another bit about my 'ability' and 'opportunities'. I just nodded at everything he said, it was easier that way.

'It's just as well your father isn't here, Tommy,' Ann was saying. She had her e-fag out, she was switching it on.

'I'm afraid we don't permit electronic cigarettes anywhere in the school or grounds, Mrs Gillyhooley.'

'But it's electric, it's not a real fag, there's no smoke.' She waved it in the air.

'Yes, I'm aware of that. But our smoking ban now extends to electrical devices as well.' Ann put the e-fag back into her handbag. 'Given you and Tommy's appearance here this morning, am I right in assuming that we can expect a vast improvement in attendance and participation for the rest of the year?' Sherlock's lip turned a bit, he might even have been smiling.

'You're going to work hard now, aren't you, Tommy?' Ann said.

'Yeah. Sure.'

'I'll bring him right to the door, Mr Sharlaton. It was the buses around the entrance, you see, that put me off. I was afraid I'd get jammed up.'

'If you come a little earlier, you shouldn't have a problem. It was nice to meet you.'

'Thank you, Principal.'

Sherlock got up, opened the door and waited for us to leave. 'You can go straight down to French, Tommy.'

Marley chewed onion rings in the Resource Area at first break. He had been on about his sudden illness since the bell went. 'It was that bug on the telly. I was in the cot the whole time.'

'I was thinking that.' I nodded, but I wouldn't look him in the eye.

'I didn't get the phone back online till this morning, and I saw you were in touch, scan. But I knew I'd see ya down here.'

'Ye going out for a quick one?' Lally said, coming up to us.

We went out by the V.P., up the concrete stairs, through the tennis courts, around the morning kick about amongst the fourth years, and down to the smoking wood. It was crowded and Lally stopped at the first gorse bush.

'I wouldn't stall here,' I said. 'Trifle can see right up the path from his office. It's a miracle more aren't caught.'

'Do you hear Tommy the boy with all the moves?' Marley pulled out twenty Benson & Hedges through his fly. 'Chillax. There's no one in the office, blinds are drawn.' We lit up. Lally saw someone he knew and left us.

'What's the story Friday?' I said, taking the chance. Lally always seemed to be stuck between us these days.

'Yeah, it's a nice motor alright.'

'We should get two grand off Eric for a yoke like that.'

'Bit close to the barracks, that house?'

'No closer than the last one.'

'Is this "America's Most Wanted" beside me?'

'I was thinking we draw your man out before the disco. Scan it and pick her up after, late on.'

'You have her all worked out.'

'Are you on for it?' I said. Marley stared at a spot on the ground, slowly tapping the ash of his fag. 'What is it?'

Marley shook himself. 'It's these tabs I'm on for the bug. They have me zonked.'

I stuck it out for the day, sitting at the back, expecting Sherlock to look in and check if I was present, but he never did. Teachers droned on as I doodled on the same first year copy I used for all subjects. Marley reckoned the bug had done something to his hearing and he sat up at the top of the class, near Rebecca. She whispered to Peter French beside her every time the teacher's back was turned.

I got a lift home with one of the other kids, a second year from The Mackon. Margaret O'Dea's hatchback was parked outside the mobile. She got out as I arrived, waved at the family that dropped me off. 'Hi, Tommy.'

'Hi. Do you know them?'

'No, just being friendly. Doesn't cost anything, you know.' I led her inside. 'I won't keep you too long. I know you'll want to get your dinner. Who's cooking?' She sat across from me on the far sofa bed. She opened her bag and slid out her laptop.

'Ann had something on this evening. I'll probably heat up a Dr Oetker.'

'A what?'

'Pizza.'

'Ah.' Her MacBook hummed as it came on. 'How was school today?'

'Fine. Do you want a cup of tea?'

'No, thank you. I don't take caffeine, remember?' She smiled. 'Since I was talking to you, my board have assessed your current living arrangements, taking into account the last two years since your dad went into prison, our talk here the other day and my meeting with your uncle, Jeremy Wall.' I thought I saw something moving through the Perspex. I tried to see beyond Margaret O'Dea, down the end of the field. I could just make out Tuohy amongst the bushes. His tractor was parked at the corner of the field. He was doing something with the barbed wire at the gap where the cattle kept breaking in. There were some new stakes on the ground. 'I know you had a meeting this morning with Mr Sherlock about your attendance. Your...Ann Gillhooley was present. Is your uncle sick?'

'It's his back. He was in Lebanon.'

'Your attendance has been very poor since the new year began, hasn't it?'

'There were a lot of free classes.' I was hungry and getting tired of it all now.

'Right. Now, my board have recommended an application for an emergency court order that will allow for your transfer to foster care until you are at least sixteen.'

'Transfer? But I'm sixteen in a few months. What's the point of—?'

'This is a critical time for you, Tommy. We don't want to see you slipping away from your schoolwork. Your Junior Cert is coming up next year. What we want to do is move you as soon as possible. We have a lovely family in Cloonloch on our list, the McCourts. I was out there this morning. They have a fine big airy bedroom ready and waiting for you. Nice comfortable study desk and chair, shelves for all your books. They have very fast Wi-Fi and great views of the town. John McCourt is a postman and his wife Wendy works from home as a copy editor. They have a son, Mark. He's fifteen, same age as yourself.' Mark: real square head name. 'You could get on really well. They live in a lovely estate of detached houses on the outskirts. You would have to transfer to Cloonloch College, but it could be a fresh start for you. What do you think?'

Margaret O'Dea had become a problem. I wouldn't look at her. I stared at dad's bed. On the duvet, one of mam's old medicine books was opened, face down: *How we die: Reflections on Life's Final Chapter*.

'It's clear to this office, Tommy, that you are completely neglected in a range of essential areas, in the sense of education, social integration, and domestic supports. And it's a real shame as Mr Sherlock has informed me that despite your poor attendance, he believes you have high academic potential.'

'Huh?'

'Basically Tommy, you have the makings of a very successful student, but you are simply not getting what you need, whether you realise it or not, not right now and not right here in this mobile home, with your father in prison for at least another two years and your mother permanently incapacitated in a nursing home.'

'But mam is on new tablets, she's getting better—'

'You are not attending school or else ducking many classes, you are camped here day and night, without any healthy stimulus. This is not an ideal environment and it could have dire consequences for you in the long term.'

'But I was in every day this week!'

'I know how clever you are, Tommy. Popping your head in for the register is not sufficient. The Principal and his V.P. are aware of this strategy amongst students.' Margaret O'Dea paused. 'Tommy, can I get a drink of water?' I poured her a glass from the drum. As I sat, I saw Tuohy at the corner of the field, trouncing the new stakes with a sledge. Margaret O'Dea sipped from the glass. 'Thank you, Tommy. Don't get me wrong. This meeting is not about criticising you. The situation you find yourself in at the moment, none of it is your fault. You deserve much better and it's true that the system has let you down, failing to address your case for a lengthy period after your father went to prison and your uncle became your legal guardian. You've been left on your own for too long—'

'Midnight and Ann—'

'I spoke to your uncle again yesterday, and he is in complete agreement in this. He has his own issues—,' I could just imagine Midnight blathering about his back and his chest and his poxy hearing to Margaret O'Dea. 'He admitted that he and Miss Gillhooley are simply not capable of supervising you, try as they have. Your uncle has signed the necessary paperwork for the transfer.'

'He's what?'

'We want to move you to the McCourts as soon as possible. It will be on trial until you are sixteen, with a monthly review, of course. But if all parties are happy, it could be extended until you are eighteen. It would be a fresh start for you, Tommy. You'd get all the home supports you need.'

Images were coming through of this alien family in Cloonloch, square heads and triangular eyes, Sunday evenings, all holding hands on a tweed sofa in front of a log fire, watching some rotten talent show, they would tuck me in later, tell me a story with a picture book, because they'd have firewalled the internet out of sight. I thought I was going to vomit all over Margaret O'Dea.

'No, no. I'd be better off here.'

'I know you think that now, Tommy. But in a few years, it'll be clear that this was the right decision.'

'But I don't see the point of it.' Margaret O'Dea looked at me, as if I'd really offended her.

'I know it will be strange at first, a new house, new school, new people around, but believe me, you won't feel settling in. You could have a great time–'

'But why are ye botherin' with this?' I felt cornered.

'The state has a duty to ensure teenagers like you don't get neglected.' I could see there was no point arguing with her. There was only one way out.

'When did you say I'll be going?' I could see the win in her eyes.

'We could go over on Saturday morning for a visit. Then if everything is alright, which I'm sure it will be, you could move in on Monday. The court order is in process, but we can transfer you in the interim, when circumstances warrant, as they obviously do in this case. This could be a new start for you, Tommy.' Margaret O'Dea spread a stack of shiny leaflets about foster homes on the table before she left.

I assembled the rifle quickly, enjoying the new skill in my hands, moving from breech to block, block to butt, fitting the telescopic sites, hooking on springs, clicking in casings and loading the magazine. I went outside, around the back, walked through the site, by the useless stumps of walls. Tuohy's tractor was gone. Two new stakes stood crookedly in the gap. It looked like he'd given up.

I aimed carelessly at the tops of branches in distant trees, then at overhead electric cables. Midnight had once shown me how to hold a weapon. He said the recoil from some guns can bruise all over your arm. It had happened him once in recruit training. There was a way to set it on the ground, like a sniper, legs flat, feet turned out, chest to the ground, and a way to set it standing, butt of rifle tight to shoulder, legs comfortably waist-width apart, left hand supporting the breech. He showed me in the mobile after some cans of Dutch Gold, using the handle of the sweeping brush as the Remington was always locked away. Dad came in during the tutorial and went mad. He said I would never fire a 'poxy rifle' or set foot in a 'dirty old barracks', fighting for 'some ol' prick of a politician'. He told us that my future was college and a job as a 'Doctor or Lawyer'.

A bird, probably one of the northerners, landed on the electric cables across the road. I found a position, lined the target up in the crosshairs. I anchored the butt at my shoulder, pulled back the bolt, clicked it forward, hearing the metallic rattle as the round slid up the breech. I switched the catch from 'S' to 'R'. I aimed at the bird. I breathed in an out. My finger crept over the trigger. Another bird joined the first one.

There was a bang from behind me. First I thought I was under fire myself and ducked for cover. Another bang, now I heard it like a thump. I went to the utility room, looked out through the crazy 'L' along the back wall.

Tuohy was back in his tractor at the gap. He had the engine running. He pulled levers, oil hissed in the hydraulics. He had finally given up the sledge and bought a shiny new post-driver, powered by the tractor's p.t.o. I watched as the silver bars lifted the next stake and placed it into position at the edge of the ditch. A mechanical hammer whacked the top with a thump. Tuohy pulled the lever, checked the post. I lit a cigarette as he pressed the lever again, the hammer thumped, sinking the end further into the ground.

It looked like I'd have to call it off. It had been over an hour since I'd made the call, told the guy I was on my way. There was still no sign of him. Usually, when Marley rang them and told them he wanted to look at their motor, they'd come straight out to get it ready, whip the good jack from the boot and put a cheapo Aldi one there instead, give the dash an extra polish. But this guy was real casual about cashing in his twenty-grand motor.

Marley had texted me after school: 'Puking up all evening. Can't do it. Bag of tricks in patio.' He'd tossed an old sports bag with the equipment in the garden. I supposed he didn't even want me calling in. I'd been standing inside the door of the Centra across the road, pretending to look at magazines, but I could feel the staff starting to notice me hanging around. My phone buzzed. It was Eric.

'What's wrong with Jake? I texted him a few times, but there was no answer.'

'He's sick, he reckons.'

'Woman. You'll have to keep the flag flyin'. Story, bud?'

'Can't get a read at the moment. So I don't know if it's on.'

'Text me when yiz are at the place, alrigh'?' The door to Number 10 opened. The guy came down the path, followed by what I guessed was his girlfriend, hauling a Henry hoover.

'I've to go.'

I ran across the road, slid out the scanner. It was like one of those giant consoles delivery men used. I stopped at the estate entrance, fag in my mouth, acted as if I was looking for a lighter. The guy had the key out, zapped it, the indicators flashed. Sometimes the signal would be blocked by radio waves or phones, but it was programmed to zone in on cars' infrared central locking. You also had a second chance when the owner locked it.

Marley's device beeped. It had scanned the code. It was now storing it in the drive. The couple started pulling out boxes from the back seat and putting them in a 151-jeep parked at the front door. The danger was that he'd get nervous about waiting all evening for a buyer that never showed and he'd box the Mercedes in for security. But there was always this problem. Every seller had newer, flashier motors to sit into. I walked into town as the device automatically copied the info to my clone transponder key.

Most of Junior Cert was at the basement disco in the Cloonloch Arms. It was all dry ice, maple floors, blinking colours, a mineral only bar, the music thumping. Lads jumped around in soft hooded tops and sneakers or sand boots, girls with glitter on their cheeks, skirts never below the knee. There were flashes of heels, shoulders and bellies bare around tight tops. I only had one can of cider in the park with Lally and a few other heads. I wanted to keep clear for later.

Rebecca and Peter French were glued to each other at one of the round tables on the upper level. Karen and Suzanne sat giggling nearby. Rebecca's followers looked better than usual. Karen had toned down her candy floss, stroked it smooth and made it blonder. She wore a pleated mini-skirt, while Suzanne had pure white short shorts with a gold belt, you could see her hip bone. Some big lad bumped into me. He looked down at me, smiling, curly black hair, goatee, brown teeth. It was the guy from the golf clubhouse. He looked a bit old for a teenage disco. 'Alright?' He smiled. 'Want anything?'

I didn't know if he was offering me a fag or a belt in the jaw. 'I'm Billy. Need anything, give us a shout, yeah? On the house for ya tonight, alright friend?' Billy slapped me lightly on the shoulder and went on to a group of girls coming off the dancefloor. I saw Rebecca had gone over to the bar. It was time for a can of Club Lemon.

'Howya Becky!' I said, arriving beside her.

'Hi Tommy!' Her voice was higher pitched than usual. Her lips were crooked, her eyes not fully open. She got two cans of orange.

'How's Pete?' I had to roar as the music had gone up a few notches. She leant forward as I repeated the question, pulled her hair back. It was light brown now, cut to her jawline. I smelt her shampoo, it was lovely. She pulled a miniature vodka from a white leather bag.

'Do you want a taste?' I waved it away. She drank from one of the cans, then topped it with some of the vodka. 'Need a buzz…so me and Peter…yeah…'. She was shouting but I missed out on most of the next sentence or two. It ended with '…not that serious, you know, Tommy.' French arrived behind her, tapped her on the shoulder, she spun around. I was cold. They shifted. French slid his hand up the back of her top under the bra strap and slowly around the front. I went down to Karen and Suzanne.

'Didn't see you two in the park?' I shouted across the table.

'Our dads don't allow us in town before the disco,' Suzanne said.

'Oh right. Roasting in here?' I said, turning to Karen.

'Steaming.'

'Do you want to get some air?'

Karen laughed. Suzanne rolled her eyes.

'I'm going to the bar,' Suzanne said. Karen got up, we held hands, she led me to the exit door.

It was nice and cool in the hotel carpark, out of the screeching beat of disco music, the lights, the shouting and laughing. There were a few other couples there already, some were just standing around, smoking. I could smell hash. Billy had found a few customers. Others were up against the wall, clamped together, knickers around knees, shirts opened, bodies grinding together, careless of onlookers. I saw some of the smokers filming the action for upload later. We went to the corner of the building, behind a rosebush planted in a bed of pea gravel. Karen lay against the wall, pulled me to her. I tried to shift her, but she kept her lips locked together. When I did manage to squeeze my tongue through, I hit a wall of clenched teeth and breath like Ribena. She drew her head back. I guessed she'd want to go straight back into the disco. I'd buy her a can of Fanta, we'd talk about school, arrange a date on Saturday in the bowling alley in Cloonloch. I wouldn't mind, I'd be happy to be with her. Karen wasn't Rebecca, but she was alright.

Karen reached into her lemon wedge handbag, pulled out a small silver package. She zipped down my fly, slickly slipping out my dick. I shivered at her touch, while loving it. I was so stiff I thought I'd burst. Karen laughed then, rolling on the johnny. I tried to act as if none of this was new to me, but I guessed she knew the truth. She'd gone commando.

I began to finger her, but she pulled my hand out of the matted wet hair, guided my lad into her. I reached up under the tiny top, squeezed my hand under the bra strap, but there were no breasts available. I eventually found a flat nipple somewhere, tweaked it as I jerked.

There was fuck all enjoyment. It felt like someone was taping my arse the whole time and it would be on Instagram within minutes. There was her Ribena breath and the way I didn't know her, not really, we had never talked, only classroom slagging, the dull shoving didn't seem to be at all enough.

I felt awful stupid to even think like that. I was getting the ride, every fifteen-year-old boy's dream. I jerked off, did get a buzz from the spill which lasted for three seconds as I filled up the rubber. I wanted to kiss her on the lips, but she shoved me back, the condom fell off, onto the ground with a splat.

Karen angled around me, walked along the hotel wall, to the exit door. The music inside still pounded, she pushed down her skirt, tidied her blouse. I stood at the rosebushes, staring.

The estate across from Centra was silent at two o'clock. The jeep was still tucked in at the front door, the CLS 300 on the edge of the drive. I ran across the common ground, hood up, clone out. I clicked the button. Like magic, the indicator lights flashed. Doors were unlocked. I got in, smooth leather seats, cool walnut fascia. He had been busy polishing her up for me, but there would be plenty of time later to admire the sheen. I plugged in the transponder clone, pressed the start button.

The engine purred into life. I calmly drove out of the estate, just another zombie head going down to the 24-hour for a packet of wine gums. I clicked on the phone app. to muffle the GPS and switched on the music centre as I took the ring road for the east. Violins, cellos and clarinets took over the car. It was classical, 'Beethoven IX' the file said. I liked it, turned it up, wound down all the windows, the night air blew through, it was electric.

I got to the Marina in two and half hours. Roads were dead as expected. There was no one around the pier. All the yachts were in darkness, just black shapes against the skyline lit with the moon, apart from the tiny flashing green alarm lights.

I stopped at Eric's warehouse and sent a text. There was no answer but that often happened when he was out for the night. Still, I rang him and left a message. The first bus left the city at five and I wanted to be on it with my money.

I got sick of waiting. The tiredness was starting to get to me, the high of the nightclub, Karen, the long drive across the country. I was seeing things moving along the water's edge that weren't there. I got out and walked by the yachts. Just like Eric had said, the only one without the alarm light was the 'Sunseeker 115'. It was a beast of a boat. I climbed over the rails onto the deck. There were three floors clad in glass and white panels. I could smell polished wood and steel.

All the doors were locked. I tried to see inside, my eyes getting used to the darkness. I saw a wall-to-wall sofa in the lounge. In the next section, there was a huge dining room, long table, cushioned chairs, chandelier overhead. At the end, a kitchen of walnut doors, marble floors, granite worktops.

I climbed up the exterior ladder, to the next level. I found a PVC door unlocked. I came into a double bedroom, king-size thick flowery duvet, golden door handles, patterned wallpaper, glass sidelights. There was a massive tiled ensuite behind with his and hers washbasins. I went up the steel spiral staircase, came into the sky deck. There was a six-man Jacuzzi, dome roof of Perspex above, stars twinkling beyond. The bar counter had a shiny Guinness tap and optics loaded with whiskies I didn't know.

A small door in a lobby area to the front led down steps to the control room. There was a huge panel under the massive windscreen: monitors, dials, buttons, a wheel for steering. I wondered if you could really hot-wire a yacht. Half a million euro in Calais. I knelt, pulled off a panel, lit up the space behind with the phone. I pulled out a thick bunch of wires. I was getting excited, I pared them back with a key. You could just touch them together to ignite the electrics. It probably wouldn't start her, but I didn't care. I did it anyway.

A light came on somewhere, a fan started whirring deep in the bowels of the yacht. There was a thump downstairs. I got up, went back to the sky deck, down the spiral staircase to the first level. As I came into the kitchen, a torch flashed into my face. I could see luminous jackets. Someone called my name.

The detectives had ditched the suits. It was a Saturday, I supposed. The bald one wore a shirt and slacks, the younger, curly-haired one was in chinos and a North Face top. I was in a room of rubber-coated walls, sitting in a plastic chair, an ID band clipped to my wrist. I'd been there for hours but I couldn't tell what time it was. They'd taken my phone away.

'Guess you're tired waiting, Tommy,' the curly-haired one said. 'I know you've had a brief chat with the Port Gardaí and we'll get you processed as soon as we can.' Processed. Sounded like something you did to canned food. 'We're from the Serious Crime Division. I'm Detective Armstrong and this is Detective O'Keefe. We're the investigating officers assigned to your case. We want to talk about what happened last night at the Marina in East Wall.' Armstrong opened one of a pile of folders in front of him. 'The guy who owns that yacht. He lives in Monaco.' Eric had been right about the Sunseeker. 'I'm afraid he is not a happy camper, Tommy. He wants to press full charges.'

'For what–,' I was croaking. I'd hardly spoken in hours.

'You need a drink of water?' Armstrong got up, left the room. O'Keefe stared at me. Armstrong came back in with three plastic cups of water.

'Now, one for everyone in the audience!'

'Thanks.' It was cold and good. 'That boat, I was just looking at it.'

'Right. See the problem with that explanation is you had a bunch of wires out, under the control panel. You had them pared back with a key. The electrics were fired up. That looks to us like a guy trying to get something running.'

'I was…'.

'Look,' Armstrong sat up, leaned on the table. 'We know it takes an expert, maybe a team of experts to operate a beast like that…'. He looked down at the folder, the sheets he'd leafed through. 'A Sunseeker 115. But when something is worth twenty odd million, you need to be sure, do you see our point?'

'I was just looking around.'

'Legally, you turned the engine. You can guess what happens when someone is caught with twenty million stolen from a bank?'

'I thought you couldn't interview a minor without a parent? Isn't that the law?'

Armstrong sat back. 'Your da is in prison, your ma is incoherent in a nursing home and your uncle won't answer his phone. We've done everything we can to get someone here for you. We know the law too, see. Legal aid is on the way. But this isn't an interview. It's a chat. We're trying to help you here.'

Armstrong closed the folder, took up another one. 'Let's forget about the yacht for a second. Now the car that was parked down at the warehouses in the Marina. The CLS 300,' he read from the folder. 'You don't deny stealing that one, do you?' He looked up at me, reaching for his pen on the table. 'That's how you got to East Wall in the first place from Cloonloch, isn't it?'

'I need the solicitor.'

'Right, right. Then there's these.' He dragged other folders to the centre, held together by a rubber band. He puffed as if he was climbing steep stairs. He took up his own water and skulled half it. O'Keefe hadn't touched his, he watched me the whole time. I tried to ignore him, looked at a point on the wall. 'Tommy? You still with us?' Armstrong waved his hand.

'Yeah.'

'Good. I thought you'd faded off there for a second. Been a long night for you. Didn't sleep much in the holding cell, did you?'

'No.'

'Breakfast?'

'Toast, yeah.'

'The staff sergeant will get you a takeaway after this. I'll organise that for ya. Curry chips, burger, coke, alright?'

'Yeah.'

Armstrong put his hands around the stack of folders. 'There were twenty-nine cars reported stolen in the Cloonloch area since this time last year. Compared to four the previous twelve months. Bit of an upsurge. Twenty-three were found burnt out in various parts of the surrounding countryside. The other six, all stolen since May, have never been recovered. Maybe that's because they're all high-end, luxury motors. Two Beamers, a 2012 and a 2013, a 2012 Lexus and three 131 Mercedes, including the one you brought last night to the Marina. Know anything about those other twenty-eight, Tommy? You and your mate stole all of them, didn't you? We're agreed on that, yeah?'

'I'll talk to my legal aid.'

'See,' Armstrong took another sip of his water, 'You could really do something for yourself here, Tommy. Listen,' he sat up again, his eyes widening. 'You watch TV? Or series on the internet, I suppose. Box sets, yeah?' I looked at the floor. 'That police drama stuff? Deals, interview techniques, good cop, bad cop, yeah? You know, it's all shite. None of that crap ever happens in the real world. For us, it's boring paperwork and computer searches most of the time. We laugh about it, don't we?' Armstrong looked over at O'Keefe who still stared at me. Armstrong laughed alone. 'Yeah, you probably guessed that, Tommy. You're smart, we know that much about you. But just this time, we could maybe do a bit of the TV stuff. Say if you were to help us resolve−,' he nodded at the pile of folders, 'these car thefts I just reminded you of. If you told us who the other guy is that was with you − I suppose you know we have two thieves on lots of street and security cams − and you gave us the devices you used and told us exactly where you got them…well.'

Armstrong put his hands behind his head, stretched himself and sat back. 'That would help you a bit. Help you a lot. You probably wouldn't be great friends with the other guy anymore, but friendship is overrated, hey?' He looked at O'Keefe, then coughed. 'You know you won't be going to jail at your age – but the alternative for juveniles – believe me, you don't even want to think about going down to Trimon Halls or Portroyal. I've seen your file. Both Social Services and the school say you're a bright kid, decent mixer, talented at art, a reader. You'll never be the same when you get out of those places. Very few graduates from there have stayed out of trouble after. We see it all the time.' Armstrong leaned across the table. 'Every one of those cars were bought by honest, hard-working people, members of your own community, people who get up every morning and go out to work, raise families, do their best. Then along comes you and your pal–'

'I didn't steal twenty-nine cars. But I know them cars were all insured. They probably got more for them in the pay-out then they were worth.' It was Marley's constant mantra every time we took a motor. 'The only ones suffering here are the rotten insurance bastards, scan. Sure they have my ol' man cleaned out.' The detectives were both scowling at me now.

'You won't get very far with that attitude, I'm afraid, Tommy.' Armstrong opened the folders, turned sheets quickly, looking for something. 'This 05 Avensis here. You took it last January. The 7th. Bored after Christmas, were ye? Owned by a woman nine months pregnant. The couple only had one car. What if she'd gone into labour? What if she'd lost the baby waiting for a taxi?

You'd have caused that child's death, sonny.' He pulled up another folder. 'Yes, that 2010 Renault Estate, in November. A seventy-year-old pensioner owned it, he had a pacemaker…what if his heart had given in? Another death on you and your mate…and this guy, George Harris, you took his 2011 Honda in April. Did you know his eight-year-old son's appendix burst the same week? Just as well they had a second car, eh?'

Armstrong looked up. 'Yeah, our Super is pretty big on crime impact stats. They help us quite a bit in court. Didn't think of all this, did you, Tommo? When ye put the hoods up and got out the coat hangers? Doesn't look so good when you put it like that, does it?' I felt like I was going to vomit. 'There is another way out of this mess. You don't even have to squeal on your friend, and if you do take it, I guarantee you'll be going straight home to the bogs,' Armstrong said. 'It really is the best solution for you, Tommy.'

'Who is the fence?' O'Keefe said, leaning forward. His voice was lower than Armstrong's. He took out a pad with the Garda crest on it and a pen and shoved them in front of me. 'Write his name there.'

'We check it's right and you go home to The Mackon,' Armstrong said. 'Simple as. He won't ever know for sure who told us. You'll still go to court. But…a juvenile, no previous, very difficult domestic circumstances, living out in an almost abandoned bog village, alone in a caravan, dad a convicted bank robber in prison long term, mam in a nursing home, incoherent, uncle, a disgraced ex-military simpleton, the suspect a significant help to Gardaí in their investigation into an

138

international luxury car theft and resale organisation. You get the idea.' He pointed to the ceiling. 'Come on, Tommy, see the light here! It's the only thing that makes sense. Either give us the fella you lifted the cars with or give us the fence. The fence is the premium option. It buys you a lot more.'

'Do you think they care about you?' O'Keefe said.

'They don't give a fuck about you,' Armstrong said.

'Think they'll be bothered about you in whatever hellhole you're put in?'

O'Keefe stood up, walked around the table. He was taller than I'd thought. I wondered would he strike me, his fist clenched at the side. He stared at me for ages. 'Just give us the fucking name.'

'I'll wait for my legal aid.'

'Bad decision, Tommy. Have it your own way,' Armstrong said. O'Keefe left the room. I raised my hands.

'Can I get these cuffs off?'

'Afraid not, son. Super's orders. Let's go.'

A man with a moustache, blue jumper with a badge reading 'steward' and a pair of grey trousers led me through a hall. He rattled a huge bunch of keys along the radiators.

'Awful time of night to be checkin' in. Why didn't they keep yiz in the barracks till Monday?' The steward nodded at a big room. 'That's the showers.' It looked a bit like the Assembly Hall in Ballincalty, with a stage blanked off, tall windows, decorated ceilings. But there was no balcony or alcove at the end. That area had been converted to a large tiled square, lines of showers, with changing benches up front. 'Better get down here early in the morning, yeah? After half seven, it gets jammers.' He tugged me along by the elbow.

'This used to be a boarding school?'

'I'm not a fuckin' history teacher. That's the metal shop arigh'?' I looked in through the toughened glass. Beyond, there were blockwork booths, a line of welders on the polished concrete floor, angle grinders and steel bars tossed around. 'If yiz are here long term, yiz'll be in there Monday and Friday mornings, arigh'? Watch out is my advice. Lots of sharp objects and angry young fellas.' He looked at his watch. 'I'm not goin' all the way down to the canteen now. Yiz'll have to follow the lads tomorrow. Breakfast is at half eight, yeah?'

At the end of the hall, there was a room with a pool table in the centre and some small desks and chairs. Three lads sat in a corner, they wore baseball caps and trackies with the ends tucked into sports socks.

'Alrigh' lads? This is O'Toole. He's checkin' in for a while.' Someone laughed. The steward looked around the door. 'Masterson, what the fuck are you doin' down here? You're not allowed in the Pool Room anymore, now get the fuck up to your bed!' A tall blonde youth, barefoot, in a white t-shirt and pyjama bottoms, came from the corner. He laughed into the steward's face.

'Hi-hu! Tool!'

'Get out of me mouth, Masterson.' The tall blonde lad smiled at me and went down the hall. The steward took my arm again. 'Come on. Upstairs.'

We climbed two flights of a creaking staircase, walked down a green carpet, damp rising on the walls. Big areas here had been subdivided. Room 15 was 12 foot by 6. There was just enough room for a bed and a locker.

'You can stick your stuff in that press. Do yiz have a phone?'

'Yeah.'

'Don't leave it here. Don't leave anything here yiz don't want lifted, alrigh'?'

'There's no lock?'

'No.'

'What about Wi-Fi?'

'What do you think this is, the Gresham?'

The steward left me at the door, shaking his head, and rattling his keys again along the radiators.

At half six the next morning, I gave up trying to sleep. I got up, got dressed, brought my bag with me down the stairs. In the shower hall, I stripped on the benches. The water was nice and warm.

As I rinsed, I felt a sharp sting on my leg. I swung around. Through the steaming water, I saw Masterson. He was naked and held a wet towel with a knot on the end of it. A bar of soap slid around in his other hand.

'Hi-hu! How's Tool!' He laughed, then whipped the towel across my thighs, the distance just so the knot razed across with full bite.

'What do you want?'

Masterson whipped the towel again, this time on my arm. 'Hi-hu! To do that, Tool!' Another whip on the stomach.

'What's your problem?'

'Tool!' Something was ringing, down at the benches. I looked beyond Masterson. It was my phone. I rushed past him, still covered in suds. 'Hi-Hu!' Masterson snapped the towel, clipping my ankle, he stepped under the still flowing water.

I found my phone in my jeans. It was dad. 'Hi.'

'Howya lad. Did I wake you up? It's the only time I can use this yoke.'

'No, I was up.'

'This is messy, Tommy.'

'I know.'

'What the hell were you doing on that yacht?'

'Just having a look.'

'Jesus Christ, she's worth millions! It looked like you were trying to hot-wire it, for fuck's sake! And the fella that owns it is a right prick!'

'I know, dad.'

'What's your legal aid like? Worse than useless, I suppose.'

'He looks around my age and I can barely understand his accent.'

'They're all just poxy trainees, them free legals. Not worth a wank. That's why I'm stuck here. If you had someone right, you might be able to get out of this on a technicality. They always make a bollocks of the paperwork somewhere along the line. All ya need is a wrong number on the arrest sheet or something. I was talking to my new brief about it. He's a good local man, one of the boys here put me on to him, he's working on me appeal for early release. But I can't bug him too much. I owe him a pile of cash already and I can't straighten him till I get out of this place.' An image came of Pock and Midnight searching the mobile the evening I'd came home early. If they'd found what they were looking for, dad would have no money to pay anyone. 'But he'll do me a favour. He'll send down his P.A. on the train. The young fella will get all the details off ya, what the detectives have been spouting off about, that kind of thing. If they've any real evidence. If my man gets all the details laid out in front of him, he might be able to do something. Abusing a juvenile in an interview or some crap like that. You'd have to fire the other fool though. What do you think?'

'Yeah. Maybe.'

'My fella is a genius at finding loopholes. He'd have nailed that prick in the van and his stories if he was in the court.'

'Who was that fella that got you locked up anyway?'

'Can't talk about it now, lad. You might know my brief's son, he goes to Ballincalty.'

'What's your solicitor's name?'

'Johnny Marley.'

'Marley? Who's the P.A.?'

'He told me he started training up his young fella during the summer. Keep him out of trouble. Maybe you know him?'

'Jake? Jake is the P.A.? Sure, he's only sixteen?'

A vision of Marley came then, in a white shirt and grey tie, folder under his arm, sitting in the visitors room, waiting for me. 'Ho-aye scan! Some maze of shite the law, huh? Now, I've been reviewing your case with the ol' man, and we think...'. Dad was still talking. 'He's training him, I don't know the ins and outs of it, do I? Look, if you did end up there for a year or two, it might not be all bad. Ann reckons you can do the Junior Cert in Trimon. One of the wardens told her. You could do it on your own, get all the books and shite brought in. You need the schooling, lad. You can't be giving up halfway like me. You weren't going in half the time on the outside anyways. It might be the best thing that ever happened you. All for luck, you know…'. Another whip of the towel, this time across my head. I swung around. Masterson stood in the doorway, dripping into a pool of water. He scratched his balls, he had an erection.

'Hi-hu! That your boyfriend, Tool!' He laughed insanely.

I went to Masterson as dad talked. I smacked the phone across his face. His blocking was shit. 'Big lads made awkward scrappers', those were the words that rang around The Mackon schoolyard, busted bloody noses, scratched hands on gravel. I made several solid, steely connections with Masterson's jaw, tears in my eyes, nose running, breathless, pieces of plastic phone shattered, dad's voice squealing as a tiny speaker spun through the air. Masterson stared blankly, he tried to move, his feet slipped on the water, he went down, his skull cracked against the tiles. 'Tommy, what the fuck is going on there?' dad's puny words came from somewhere. I jumped across Masterson, blood poured through his smooth blonde strands. I wanted to break him, to do real damage, to silence him for good.

144

Lights flashed, bodies jerked. Dry ice rolled in huge clouds. I pushed through leaping revellers, sweat and perfume in the air, the beat-beat-beat of music thumping. I sipped on a Bud, my first of the night. I needed a clear head when I was working. I found Karen and Suzanne at the exit door. Karen kissed me on the cheek as she slipped a twenty into my hand. I dropped a tiny plastic package into her black handbag. There were cameras everywhere, inside the pubs and clubs all over Cloonloch, outside on the streets. The film was never watched unless there was an incident, but I was still careful. I avoided obvious places like carparks, the industrial estates, the bowling alley. I hid in plain sight, everyone knew it was the only way I'd do business.

I had covered the basement crowd by around 1. About half the packets were sold, it had been quiet. The summer was over, kids back at school, full-time jobs became part-time or stopped altogether under the pressure of new year studies. Even so, I had still made a profit.

It was time to go, late night business was erratic, buyers became pissed and loud. The last thing you wanted was some fool shouting on the path about value for money or getting back the wrong change. That sort of thing didn't end well. It had happened before.

Once I knew I was finished, I couldn't wait to get out of there, get home, chill out. I rarely bothered with a spliff myself. I didn't like the out of control feeling. I'd have a bottle of lager and an hour of Beethoven, blaring out the door. I hated the discos and late bars, the rubbish music, shite talk, fake hugging.

Rebecca was alone at the main exit. She'd been chatty anytime I'd ran into her during the disco, although she wasn't a customer. She seemed to get enough of a buzz out of the alcopops she sucked on. She'd shaved her head over the summer. There was now just a smooth black sheet of hair around her scalp. It made her brown eyes even bigger. She wore a leather mini-skirt, tight buttoned-up top, she was scrolling on her phone.

I wasn't sure about her new image, but it wasn't her looks I fancied really, once I'd gotten to know her. It was more her way, the way she'd been when we were in first year, outside O'Malley's, having ice-cream, chilling. 'Hey, Beck!'

'Heeeeyyyyy!' Her eyes were droopy. She linked my arm as we went outside, stopped once we got past the herd of bouncers. She pulled a miniature Smirnoff from her white handbag, offered me a taste.

'No thanks, I don't drink that stuff.'

'On the dry are ya?'

'Working.'

'Working? Right, right, Tommy.' She winked at me sloppily.

'Where's Peter tonight?'

'That's all in the paaast. Fuckin' dick that fella. Sooo, what sorta night yave, Tommy?' She swung around on my arm, her breath of raspberry alcopop, her hand slid over my balls, long painted nails. 'Getting a taxi?' she whispered.

On the sofa bed, she pulled off my t-shirt, stroked my chest, still bare as the day I was born. None of the creams I'd bought on the internet had encouraged hair to grow. It didn't bother me this night though, I was finally getting with Rebecca. 'Soooo…why are you…you know…how did you get into…,' she raised her hands, made her fingers nod, '"working".'

'Handy money. Lads…you know…in that place I was, it was their mate…'. We kissed in between our words. I opened the buttons of her top, she helped me take it off. I couldn't help jaw-dropping at the lacy black bra underneath. 'Yeah, their mate…he was working in Cloonloch…then he went away.' I unhooked the strap, the tits spilled out. I buried my head between them.

'Mmm…they trust you, Tommy…so quick?'

I let her nipple slide out of my mouth. 'Sure they do. I'm trustworthy.' I smiled. We shifted again. I gave all her teeth a tongue polish.

'When did you get out?'

'June.'

'Sintense.' I was naked on the sofa bed as I slid off her mini-skirt and knickers all together. 'You're a baaad boy, Tommy O'Toole!' Rebecca laughed as she rolled the condom down on me.

The coughing was deep, pained. There was spitting and moaning. I could smell blood. I went down the hall and pulled the door open.

'Get out Tommy! Go on up to the kitchen,' dad said, his shirt open, his hands holding mam's hair back, she was in pyjamas, her fingers covered in vomit around the rim of the toilet. I ran up to the kitchen, somebody snored beside me.

I opened my eyes. It was awkward on the sofa bed, but I couldn't be bothered clearing all the books and boxes off dad's double duvet when we got back to the mobile.

I was facing Rebecca. I watched her chest heave in and out. Her make-up had faded, her breath was sour. She moaned and turned to me, eyes closed, she kissed me open-mouthed. I tried to angle myself over her, her hand slid down my dick. The blanket slid off us onto the floor, a draught passed over my arse. There was a clink of metal behind me. I swung around.

Midnight pulled the end of his ignition key out of an earhole. Pock sat next to him on the sofa bed across, scratching a massive boil red raw on his ankle.

'Jesus! What the fuck!' I shouted, sitting up, grabbing my boxers.

'Not interrupting ye, are we?' Pock said, taking out a box of Purple Silk Cut. I pulled on my jeans, threw the blanket over Rebecca.

'How long are ye here?'

'Don't worry, we didn't see anything. The door was open. Your uncle reckoned we'd have to get here early to catch up with ya. Seems like you're a busy man these days.'

'We need to talk to ya, Tommy,' Midnight said, searching his pockets.

'Could ye go outside for a minute until we get organised?'

Rebecca screamed into my ear, right up the lobe, I felt the drum rattle. She pulled the blanket around her, grabbed her knickers off the middle of the table, skirt and top from the floor and ran down to the toilet, breasts bouncing. Pock stared at her the whole time. Midnight scanned his dirty fingernails. Rebecca banged the toilet door, we heard a splash.

'What's this about, Midnight?'

'You know Paddy here, Paddy Rock...'. Midnight ran his hand through his greying curls, scattering clouds of dandruff everywhere. He had a King Edward out, unwrapped it. 'We were in Leb. together. He came down last night. He wanted a quick word with ya.'

'A word about what?' The toilet door opened. Rebecca had her top and skirt on, but they looked funny. I wasn't sure why, the skirt might have been back to front. She tossed the blanket to the floor, looked around like she was lost. I found her shoes under the table, handed them to her. 'You alright, Beck? You've gone real pale?'

Rebecca looked at the shoes, like she didn't recognise them. She ran back into the toilet, we heard her puke into the bowl.

'Oooooh,' Midnight said. 'Make you want to throw up yourself, that craic! Ugh!'

The toilet flushed again. Rebecca came out. She was slightly bent over, rubbed her stomach, specks of vomit clung to the top.

'Is there water?' She sounded hoarse. I pulled the five-litre drum out, half-filled a pint glass. Her fingers shook as she took it, gulped some down. She looked at me. 'I need my phone…where is my phone, my phone, you know?'

'Just there on the table.'

'My mother, I need to call my mother, you know? Right now, you know?' She went outside with the phone.

'Livin' the high life, eh son?' Pock said, tapping ashes on the floor.

'There's an ashtray right there,' I pointed at the table.

'I got a call from Joe's brief yesterday,' Midnight said. 'Joe got a date. He's comin' home to The Mackon next Friday morning.'

'Next Friday?' I didn't know whether to be happy or sad.

'Eight o'clock in the morning. He even has a Garda escort.' Midnight puffed. 'Look Tommy, things'll be changing around here when your ol' fella gets out.'

'So? Why do ye care?'

'This stuff you're at.'

'What?'

'If he hears about…'.

'About Beck? Don't give a fuck.'

'Act the bollocks now if you want. I'm not on about your woman.'

'Look,' Pock said, sitting up. 'We haven't time for this arsin' about. I didn't come down here to stop any man from makin' a few quid. We all have bills to pay. And as for the law, sure that's the crookedest sham of the lot.

Meself and your uncle know that better than anyone. We spent long enough in forty-degree heat, trying to stop fellas from killing each other, keep law and order in the middle of a war zone. And for what? So another bunch of pricks could run it into the ground anyway.'

'True, true,' Midnight said, nodding.

'I've no care about your stuff, if you can keep it from your old man when he's here…'.

Through the Perspex, I saw Rebecca, arms folded, walking around in a circle at the side of the road.

'It's a bad game to be in though,' Midnight said. 'You should get the hell away from it while you still can. If your poor mother knew …'.

'Aye, true that,' Pock said, nodding. 'You should listen to your uncle, if you're wise. It's one thing whipping a few motors. But that craic…never ends well.' They both sat back, Pock eventually found the ashtray and stubbed out his fag. 'Look, we just need a bit of a dig out.'

'Huh?' I wondered had they both just gone insane. 'I have about a grand here,' I said. 'Your car out there must be worth at least twenty. If you want, I can tell ye where to cash it in fair quick.'

They both laughed.

'I bet you can.' Pock was smiling. 'No, I'm not looking for a loan off ya.'

'What then?'

Pock looked at Midnight.

'Where did Joe stash that money, Tommy?' my uncle said.

'What money?'

'The ATM money, what other money!'

'How the hell would I know that?'

'Don't be a smart cunt, good lad!' Pock said. The smile was gone and he sounded pissed off now.

'I don't know where it is, he never told me.'

'Come on Tommy, don't be bullshitting us! How else did you get into selling that stuff? You don't get the start with them boys without a connection or a big lump,' Midnight said.

'What has that got to do with you?

'He must have told you, now where is it?'

'No, he didn't! Did he not tell you, Midnight?'

Midnight's face changed from his usual toothache look to a mad frown. He dropped his cigar, dived across the table, grabbed me by the shoulder, growling.

'No, he didn't tell me, you little prick!' Midnight's grip was real tight. I couldn't push him off, he was stronger than I'd thought. I hadn't seen him this mad since I spilt the oil in someone's backyard two years before. He switched his hold to around my neck, his eyes foggy, mouth shut tight. He was going in for the kill.

'Jesus Christ, Midnight!' I heard Pock shout from behind. Midnight's fingers were around my windpipe. I was choking. Pock swung him away. They waltzed awkwardly toward the door.

'Come on, come on! We'll let him stew on it!' We'll be back tomorrow morning, son! You don't want your father hearing about your shit, do ya?'

As they got out to the Audi, Midnight shook off Pock's grip. He was still panting. He nodded at Pock who got into the car. Rebecca was sitting on the ditch, head between knees, she never looked up. Midnight came slowly back to the door.

'Tommy?' I came out.

'What the fuck is going on?'

'He said he'd talk to the cops again, tell them I was involved as well if I didn't help him get it.' Midnight was whispering.

'Involved in what? Selling dope?'

'No, ya cunt! The ATM! I had to bring him out. He landed last night. Joe's release has put the wind up him to get his cash.'

'What, sure it's only dad's share?'

'We never split it. Joe has the lot. He kept it the day we were at the Castle putting the truck into the swamp. It was just for the time being, aright? We didn't know what was goin' to happen. I thought he'd shoot me last night. I told him you probably knew nothing about it. He reckoned you must have got some of it to get in with them dope crowd.' He nodded at the Audi. 'You don't know what you're dealing with there. I seen him do things in Leb....'.

'Tell the cops you were involved...'. I tried to make sense of Midnight's mutterings. 'What do you mean "again"? You mean it was Pock set dad up? But why? Wasn't it some young lad?' I thought of the Remington right behind me over the cooker. Since I'd got home, I often put it together, fired a few shots into the cottage, took it apart, polished it with gun oil. I'd ordered more rounds off the internet. Midnight patted his forehead with a screwed-up ball of toilet paper he'd pulled from his jacket.

'He had no choice but to do Joe. It's a long story. I'll tell ya again. You were too young that time.'

154

'Tell me about it now.'

But Midnight had again stopped listening to me. 'And then you make him think I know where the money is!' Midnight's lip was shivering. I thought he might have a stroke. 'If that buck out there thinks Joe gave me the ATM money and I wouldn't tell him…he's cold, that bastard.' Pock beeped the horn. 'Look, Tommy, ring Joe. Tell him you're under fierce pressure. You need a few quid. We have to get it in the morning. No tellin' what Pock will do next. It's not in the mobile or down there in them bits of houses. It's not out in The Castle either, we were through all that. It must be buried in one of the fields around here. He'd have had no time to put it anywhere else. The cops checked his car, so it's not there. Get it for him and we'll sort something out when Joe gets back.'

'You mean he's taking the lot? Pock wants to get it all before dad comes home? Nice work, Uncle Jeremy.'

'What choice do I have?'

'I thought Pock was gone abroad?'

'He came back a few months ago. His young fella is playing fuck as well. Just get Joe to tell you where it is, for the love of God, Tommy.' A car pulled up. I thought it must be Rebecca's mother, but when I looked at the ditch, she was gone. It was a Nissan hatchback. Pock stared at it blankly. I saw someone within, waving at him. It was Margaret O'Dea.

155

Margaret O'Dea sat across from me. She looked around, the place was a mess, but I didn't care. She spread out a few leaflets as the MacBook hummed. 'Just some more info on pursuits that might interest you now or later, Tommy.'

'Do you want a cup of tea?'

Margaret O'Dea smiled. 'No thank you, Tommy. The reason I'm here is we got an email yesterday from your dad's lawyer that he is to be released next Friday. You probably already got the news from your uncle.' And a lot more. 'I met with Jeremy yesterday evening and I just wanted to debrief you on the situation. As dad's coming back now and you'll be eighteen in a couple of months, my board are taking you off my list. I only deal with juveniles, you see. You are moving into the adult system. This doesn't mean you can't get in touch, should you need to. In fact, I hope that you do give me a ring, alright?' She smiled and slid her card across. 'So how have things been since last time? Early August, wasn't it?'

'Fine.'

'Mr Sherlock tells me you agreed to start back in Junior Cert?'

'He told me I had to do it.'

'It was the right move, I think, Tommy. You might have been under too much undue pressure with the Leaving Cert next summer. It's not that you aren't clever enough. But even the brightest people should learn the basics. It's the truly intelligent that know just how little they know.' I took out my Majors. Margaret O'Dea nodded. 'Ah, Majors.'

'Do you want one?'

'No, no. I...I gave up three years ago.'

'Hard?'

'Awful. Much easier never to start.' I lit up. Margaret O'Dea fidgeted and looked at books on the table I'd taken out of the library. 'I see you're doing some private reading. That's great. There could be a career path in that.'

'It's just stuff my art teacher said to read. For the exam.'

'Oh yes, I heard you're doing very well in the Art Room.'

'It's not hard when everyone else is two years younger.'

'Art doesn't always work like that, I believe.'

After Margaret O'Dea left, I cooked scrambled eggs. As I stirred them around in the pot, my body shook. My mind was racing, the ATM raid, Pock and Midnight — laughing army buddies — dad rotting away in a cell for the past four years because of some young fella somehow connected to the whole thing.

I got hot as I sat down to eat, the more I thought the less I could, it was like I was getting embarrassed or something, like maybe everything wrong in the whole world was somehow my fault. I'd only taken a few forkfuls and I had to throw the rest in the bin, couldn't look at it. It seemed to me then that everything in the mobile was dirty and sticky, like I couldn't breathe. I scrubbed the plate clean, then washed all the other plates, cups, knives, forks, spoons, glasses, hacked off the dried in food, broke one plate doing that. I cleaned down the draining board with thick suds. I pulled out a roll of rubbish bags Ann had brought, started filling one with pizza boxes, fag packets, butts from the ashtray, loaf papers, milk cartons, takeaway trays.

Soon, there were three bags of rubbish outside. I filled another sack with dirty washing tossed all around the place, socks, t-shirts, boxers. I tied up the top, left it at the door for Ann to collect. I swept the floor, pulled a can of air freshener from the press under the sink, piped it everywhere.

I sat at the table, lit a fag, my fingers were shaking. My eyes traced the outlines of the sofa bed, across to the cavity behind the cooker and fridge, under dad's bed, down along by the shower and toilet. I looked up at the press over the cooker. I got out the keys, opened it. I pulled out all the parts of the Remington, the extra boxes of rounds, set everything on the table.

During the cleaning, I'd found the old sports bag Marley had left out for me on the patio the night I'd been canned. The cops had taken the scanner away, but the bag had somehow found its way back into my belongings when I was checking out of Trimon Halls.

I put the parts of the weapon inside the bag. I got down on my knees, reached under the sofa bed. There were two small sandwich boxes taped to the steel frame. One had over a thousand in cash. I took three hundred, everything was in twenties. The other was half full of plastic packets of dope. There were about forty packets, eight hundred's worth: overflow. The guy brought the same amount for the same money every week, even though I often didn't sell everything. I took them all and put them in the bag.

I always met the guy in Groake's pub, an old man's pisshouse on the corner of the main street in Cloonloch. Blinds were drawn down in every window, killing off the daylight. There was a smell of damp and porter, cleaning fluid in the toilets and stale puke. A man with fuzzy grey hair round his ears and a few strands across the top sat on a stool behind the counter scrolling on his smartphone. Three men were perched along the bar, they all looked the wrong side of pension age. I left Marley's bag under my stool at the end, heard the Remington clink.

As I sipped my pint, I played with the beermat, tearing the bits off it, flicking them on the ground. I tried to do this without the barman noticing, which wasn't difficult. The local radio was on low. The barflies hardly spoke, one leafed through a tabloid, another slowly counted cigarettes, a third stared blankly, sniffing every few seconds. When any of them said something, it seemed like it was important, the way it crashed through the quiet, but it nearly always was no more than another drink order, just a grunt and a nod.

By half six, the guy was very late. It was strange. I rang him as I smoked at the entrance.

'Yeah?'

'It's Cloonloch.'

'Story bud. Meant to ring yiz.'

'You comin'?'

'No.'

'No?'

'Not on, arigh'?'

'How's that?'

'Billy is back. Got a date. Next Friday. I've to wait for him is what I was told.'

'He got a date? To be released?' The parole board had been busy. 'But where does that leave me? I thought he was in for another few…hello? Hello?'

I tried ringing him back. No answer. I tried again. Straight to voicemail. There was a snigger and an outbreak of laughter inside. I looked back, one of the three men was pointing at a spot on the wall over a bricked-up fireplace, the other two peered across. 'It was you did that Paddy, in 07, I'm tellin' ya!'

'In me arse!'

The ragged laughter dragged on. I looked down at Marley's bag. I could go to the toilet with it, assemble the Remington, fill the mag. I could press rounds down onto the spring-loaded panel, change the lever from 'S' to 'R'. I could come back into the bar with the rifle at my shoulder. I wondered what it would be like to shoot a living breathing

thing, squeezing the trigger, a round hurtling out, smashing through a skull, shutting down the thinking mind for good.

My phone buzzed: a text. I breathed deeply. It had to be the guy. It was a wind-up and a nasty one at that, of course it was, I saw that now. It was just too much of a coincidence that Billy was getting out the same day as dad. But it was Rebecca.

Her photo was on the screen. It had been taken back when she'd had long blonde hair, when she'd called herself 'Rebecca', when I'd really gotten stuck on her way of talking, of laughing, of being. I stared at it, before dragging to text. 'In town?'

'Yes.'

'Mum will drop me at Arms Lounge. Half nine.' I wondered how she'd managed to swing that one after this morning.

'Sound.'

Smiley face.

I had a steak with peppered sauce and a few more pints in Valentine's, one of the more upmarket pubs in the main street. By nine, when I headed down to the hotel, I was on the way to being well polished.

Many of the town's under-aged drinkers took advantage of recently finished Leaving Certs working behind the counter in the hotel lounge. They could get served in comfort without being hassled for ID cards and then stumble down the steps to the disco at half eleven. It was packed, a local three-piece played on a half-moon stage in the corner. Girls tried to look more grown-up in here, the mature setting and all, shouldered tops, trousers or long skirts, even sandals on some of them. Still they went for the kiddish mint alcopops, served by the black-shirted pimpled bar staff zipping around behind chrome-lined counters. I pushed through the flashing lights, around soft shaped figures in collared t-shirts, dark combat trousers and Timberland boots. Lads roared with laughter, patted each other on the back, bits of drunken chat rose to the suspended ceiling panels and aluminium square lights, the topics: sport, school, talent, muffled by the thumping music. I searched for the Ballincalty heads. I was a bit too woozy. I'd reached my fill, decided to start with sparkling water to dilute myself a bit. I shouldered up Marley's bag.

I spotted Rebecca in a corner with Karen, Suzanne and some other Leaving Cert girls. Rebecca was drinking what looked like orange juice. She'd made a serious effort, maybe she thought she had to after the morning. She wore thigh high black leather boots, laced up, pleated check skirt, and white top, large gold earrings. I thought maybe she just couldn't get a real drink dressed like that. She smiled at me as I neared them.

The noise was brutal. I had to turn my head to hear her. She'd felt 'awful all day', she'd been 'in bed most of it', her mum was 'furious' with her, but Rebecca 'actually agreed', she really did 'have to cop on', she was doing the Leaving Cert this year. It reminded me of the mess I was in at the school, in classes with fifteen-year-olds. I finished the water and shouted for a double brandy.

When the band finally took a break, I could at least hear what the others were saying.

'Were you training?' Karen said.

'In the gym for a while. Joined last week. Came straight out after.'

'Sport's a great idea,' Rebecca said, nodding, sipping her Britvic 55. 'Drinking and smoking lads, they're not great in the long run.' She looked at their bottles of cider, West Coast Cooler, toothpaste coloured hooch. 'I haven't had a fag all day and I'm never drinking again. The way I felt this morning was hell. I'm still dying. This orange is making me feel worse.'

'Really Beck, you're still sick?' Suzanne said.

'Yeah-hah! My head's pounding and my stomach is turning. I'm even shaking. It's awful.'

'You just need the hair of the dog,' Karen said and laughed.

'Jake not out with ya tonight, Tommy?' Suzanne said.

'Haven't seen that man for a couple of weeks.'

'Yeah, he hasn't been at school much.'

'Reckons he's studying at home.'

'How's it going in 3rd year?'

'Just kids most of them.'

'Tommy is doing a project. Show them Tommy! It's on his phone.'

'Stop it, Beck.'

'Go on.'

'What is it?'

'It's this exhibition they're putting on next week. Tommy is working on a huge painting since he started back. Mr Coyne wanted him to do it.'

'Cool.'

'Show them.'

'Nah.' The barman came over to us, acne around his chin.

'Who ordered six tequilas?'

'Here Beck,' Karen said, passing one of the shot glasses to Rebecca. 'Get that down ya, it'll sort ya out. That Britvic would kill ya.'

We left the hotel just after eleven. We walked up the street toward the taxi rank, but we kept stopping to shift or wander in and out of pubs in the process of closing their doors. Rebecca bought a naggin of vodka in an off-licence. We drank it and skinned up a doobie in the bowling alley carpark. Back down the street at Valentine's, a taxi pulled up in front of us.

'There's our lift to The Mackon!' I said. The driver got out, left the engine running, he ran into Valentine's.

'Heeeee...hee-hee! Heee's probably collecting someone...'.

'Nah, he's gettin' fags, I'd say, come on!' Rebecca got in the back seat. I sat in front. It was a Vectra, like dad's old car. He had the local radio blaring adverts. I switched it off. Rebecca looked up. 'Don't think you're supposed to do that...'.

I had my phone out, clicked on 'Beethoven IX', went straight to the 2nd movement.

'Helloo Tommy? I think you're in the wrong seat.'

So I was. I put the car in gear and drove. At the end of the street, I swung in through the Tesco car park and came out at the industrial estate.

'What the hellabella are you doing, Tommy O'Toole?' Rebecca said, as I pulled up.

'Can ya drive?'

'Sure I can drive, man, but what about the taxi man guy?'

'We don't have much time. Let's go.'

I assembled the Remington as Rebecca clipped wings and mirrors all across town. 'Turn right here.' I clicked on the loaded mag. Rebecca glanced at the gun.

'What you got there, Tommy?'

We ran by a red light, swerved around a van. 'Watch the poxy road!'

I wound the window as the van blew at us. The music boomed into the night. I cocked the rifle, cold air filled the car. 'Turn left into that estate.' We turned and passed by small detached houses, a raised green to our right.

'Tommy? What are you doing with the rifle?'

'Stop here.' We were outside Midnight's. I switched the safety catch to 'A', as we hit the kerb. I lined up the spare room in the cross hairs. The light was off.

'Man, you could hit someone…'.

The chorus of trombones blared as I squeezed the trigger, expelling 24 rounds in 8 seconds. Midnight's window shattered. Pock was in the doorway watching as we doughnut tracked out of the estate.

The taxi slowly sank into the boggy swamp at the back of The Castle. I sat with Rebecca on a big stone, watching it disappear.

'Sintense,' Rebecca said. I took out my phone, cleared my throat.

'Cloonloch Gardai?'

'Good evening. This is Jimmy Maloney, from 27 Greenhills Estate...yes...right where the shooting was, that's why I'm ringing...I don't see any of your personnel here...how much more of this thuggery do we have to take, sir? What are we paying our taxes for, hmm? Where are your detectives, I don't see them? Do you know that this town has a very serious drug problem...do you? I believe there are teenagers selling cannabis in the underage disco! Drive-by shootings, is that what it has come to now, sir? Are we supposed to accept this type of thing? Do you know what I witnessed earlier today? There is a man staying in that house with a simpleton called Wall. This thug is from up the country and drives a big Audi...I actually saw this man put packets of what I believe to be cannabis in broad daylight into the boot of his car. I'm certain they are still there. Hundreds of small packets...do you know I have three small children, is this how you police the area, is it? Do you hear me? Now, what are you going to do about it, hmm? What are you going to do?'

Tuohy's jeep skidded, even though he was only doing 20k. The way he'd hammered the brakes made me jerk forward, the tyres rolled up on the footpath. He stared at me, lollipop in mouth as we came to a standstill. 'Takes a while to get used to driving her I suppose,' I said, getting out, the Death Notices finally wrapping up. 'Fine motor, though. Well wear. Thanks for the lift, Jack.'

Maurice straightened his tie and wiped the counter with a J cloth as customers queued up. 'All set for the Leaving, Tommy?' he said, as I paid for a bag of mini rolls.

'I'm doing the Junior.'

'Doing the Junior? How come? Ah, hello Mrs Kinneally, how are you today?'

'Maurice, so sorry again about Gerald. That was a lovely speech you made in the church.'

'Ah, thank you, Mrs Kinneally, thank you. You're trying out some of our fresh store bakery, I see!'

Someone ran up behind me as I walked up the avenue. It was a heavy blonde first year, the type of lad Leaving Certs loved giving a good clatter.

'Tommy!' He wheezed as he reached me. He took out an inhaler, and I had to wait until he'd given himself a few puffs and got his breath back. 'I heard you could fix me up.'

'Wha?'

'Good skunk?'

'Who told you that, you little prick?' I grabbed him by the shoulders.

'The...the lads in Junior Cert...ow! They were in the basement of the Arms hotel, Friday night...said you were the man to see...ow!' I tightened my grip. I couldn't believe the cheek of him.

'It's my birthday, this week, I'm fourteen...'. He pulled out a twenty. 'We all chipped in.'

'Put that away, for fuck's sake!' I looked up and down the avenue. There didn't seem to be anyone watching amongst the students on the way up to school. The boy stared at me for a couple of seconds and ran off.

At the poplar island, I veered to the left, as me and Marley had learnt quickly to do in first year. Skip over the fence at the corner of the old convent building, run down by the football pitch, avoid the main corridors, Maurice and his head-slapping, nipple-tweaking friends. But this morning I pushed in the green door and went through the corridor where we'd been dragged on our first day at Ballincalty Secondary.

I took my time, reading many of the legends scraped into the white washed plaster, probably with the point of a protractor rarely used for geometry: 'LFC', 'CUNT', 'SHERLOCK IS A FAGGOT', 'JIMMY BYRNE WOZ ERE 4-10-93', with 'LIKES BOYS' added later below. Near a switch, I saw familiar names, 'J MARLEY + J OTOOLE OWN THIS HALL YOU OWE TOLL 4-10-89'. There was a splash somewhere, I knew instantly what it was.

The air was fresh in the courtyard. There was some movement in the Wet Room. I stopped at the doorway. Some fourth years stood around the cubicle, one with red hair held a small figure by the neck. The place was just the same, small cracked window, combed texture of filthy grout where tiles had fallen. The floor black with layers of ancient piss as users had gradually backed away from the channel along the wall, nearer the door, until new toilets were built somewhere else.

The fourth years looked around, then smiled. They spread out a little, like they were inviting me into their game. 'Howya Tommy!'

'We have a squealer,' the red-haired boy said. 'Told Sherlock where we were smoking. Three of us suspended for a week. Can't have that, can we?'

'Let him go,' I said. 'This game is over.' The smiles faded.

'Fuck you, O'Toole!'

I smacked the red-haired boy on the jaw, my fingers only partly fisted. He still went down howling, though. He didn't have the wiry, if foggy, resolve of a late-night raver, half stoned already, arguing over a fiver. A client like that wouldn't even register the first slap. The rest of the fourth years ran out.

'Fuck you pothead!' the red-haired roared, tight along the wall, escaping my reach. But I was glad I hadn't caught him as he ran across the courtyard.

The first year had already been ducked once, his jaws dripped with what I knew was piss. There was a big stain on the fly of his trousers.

'Thanks,' he said, as he got up off his knees.

'Go on, watch your step with them pricks.'

'I will,' he stopped at the door. 'Em…do you sell funny fags?'

'Just get the fuck, will ya?' I stood over the toilet bowl as his footsteps faded down the hall. I wondered how many first years had been shoved into the pot since dad and Marley's ol' lad were charging a tax for first years to use the corridor and avoid the Leaving Cert threat.

The Wet Room hadn't seemed to do Jake much harm. He was serious now about becoming a solicitor. 'Some maze of shite the law, scan, better than any PS4 game.' I was the one thrown into a youth detention centre for nearly two years, and I hadn't been ducked at all, thanks to someone whose name I couldn't even remember.

I rammed my heel against the rim. It rocked slightly. I went back out into the courtyard, found a big lump of windowsill, hacked off by some long-gone vandal. Most of the ceramic mould of the bog came away in pieces as I battered it. I pulled off the bottom of the bowl. Water flowed around the floor, all that was left was the dirty end of a sewer pipe. I tossed the smashed pieces in the courtyard, so everyone would know. The Wet Room was closed.

Most of Junior Cert art class were at their desks, painting A3 posters for a special exhibition at the end of the week. It was the first in a series of school fundraisers to renovate the convent section of the building. Mr Coyne stood beside me, scratching his moustache, as I worked in a corner. 'That's almost there, Tommy. It has really come on.'

He'd wanted me to do a piece on a wall panel that could be wheeled up to the Assembly Hall on the day. I was inking the orange matchstick legs of a flock of birds. They were all landing on the school avenue where lots of bread crusts were scattered. I didn't know what breed they were. I thought they might be northern migrants. They were like crows, black with flecks of grey and white. My original idea had been to paint just one bird landing, but the scene seemed too empty and I'd added twenty more, all hitting the ground at the same time. It had come out fairly well.

'Really promising. Definitely the centrepiece of the Junior Cert exhibition this one. Did you invite all your family to come, Tommy?'

'It's open to the public, sir?'

'Of course, that's the whole point. I think they'll want to see this.' There was a knock at the door. Sherlock looked in.

'Mr Coyne, can I take Tommy O'Toole please?'

'Certainly, Principal. Is it for the two classes?'

'I would think so, Mr Coyne.'

'Very well. Tommy, you can tidy this up on Wednesday. There's not much to do, it's nearly there. Some of the others will wash your brushes. You better go, you can leave your apron on the chair.'

'Some gentlemen here to see you,' Sherlock said, as we walked to his office. I was taller than him now.

171

O'Keefe and Armstrong stood at the radiator beside Sherlock's office like many students before, as though they were in trouble. But they weren't wearing blue uniforms, they were back in their sharp grey suits again. Sherlock pulled out his bunch of keys, opened the door. 'Sorry Detectives, this is the only space I have available at the moment which is fairly discreet and you won't be disturbed.'

'I'm sure it's fine, Principal,' Armstrong said, as we followed him in.

'Take as long as you need.' Sherlock left, shutting the door behind him. For once I was sorry to see him go.

The detectives walked around the desk, took Sherlock's leather seat and the swiveller which had been parked beside it. I was left with the hard chair at the front.

'Sorry to pull you from your studies, Tommy,' Armstrong said, opening his folder. 'But we just needed a quick chat...school going well? Glad to be back in "gen. pop."?' He laughed metallically. 'Dad back on Friday?'

'Is this an interview? Because–'

'No, that wouldn't be constitutional, as you know. This is just a friendly chat. We know you, you know us. We won't keep you too long. The Super just wanted us to put a few things to you.' Armstrong took up his pen. 'It's about what happened at your uncle's Saturday night.'

I could feel my skin heating up. This was not good. 'Do ye know who did it?'

'Not yet. We have one suspect. It was a rotten thing to do. The place is full of children. Any of them could've been hit. Anything you want to tell us straight up, Tommy?'

'Like what?'

'Where were you on Saturday night?'

'I didn't do anything wrong.'

'No one is saying you did. Where were you?'

'I was in Cloonloch. In the Arms.'

He wrote this down. 'Who with?'

'Few lads from school.' I named off the few squareheads that were in the Arms, like Peter French. The type I would really enjoy watching being called up to the office and grilled by detectives.

'Bit young for the Arms, aren't ye?'

'Not really.'

'There all night?'

'More or less.'

'From when?'

'Nineish.'

'Until?'

'About half eleven. Everyone else went downstairs to the nightclub.'

'I see. But you left.'

'Don't like discos really.'

'This would have been about a half hour before the incident.'

'Was it?'

'Pity you didn't go to the disco. Where did you go after you left the hotel?'

'Home.'

'Taxi?'

'Nah, I was broke. Thumbed it. Couple of lifts to Ballincalty. Then I walked out to The Mackon.'

'Two lifts? Let's have the car details, please.' They were really digging in their heels. I was making it up as I went along. It was tricky.

'I had a few...'. I said. O'Keefe glared at me.

'Really? You're seventeen, isn't it?' Armstrong said. 'Tell me about the cars, Tommy.'

'It was a green Vectra and a...red Corolla.'

'Number plates?'

'No. Sorry.'

'Someone as expert as you are at plates?' Armstrong smiled weakly. 'I'm disappointed. Who drove?'

'Who drove which?'

'The green corolla.'

'Red corolla. A woman.'

'Age?'

'Couldn't tell ya. I took no notice.'

'You sat in the front seat, yeah?'

'Yeah.'

'And you have no idea what age she was? Was she nearer to twenty or to seventy?'

'I don't know. I was out of it.'

'Who drove the other car, the red Vectra?'

'Green Vectra. A man. I don't know anymore. I was pasted.'

'Tell me again about the blue Corolla, who did you say was driving?' He was trying so hard to nail me, it was easy.

'Red Corolla. A woman, that's all I know.'

'This is unfortunate, Tommy. Very unfortunate you don't have more details on these people. If they could corroborate your story, we could rule you out of the shooting.'

'You surely don't think I did that?'

'You know this Paddy Rock character?'

'Not really.'

'But you know of him?'

'He was in the army with Midnight, yeah.'

'That's your uncle, Jeremy Wall?'

'Yeah.'

'Mr Rock was in your uncle's house at the time of the shooting.'

'So?'

'What else do you know of Mr Rock?'

'Nothing.'

'You mean you don't know it's likely he was instrumental in the conviction of your father four years ago?'

'Was he? I wasn't in the court. I was too young. They never told me how it all played out. I just know he's not been around.'

'The way it played out was Paddy Rock's son got pulled carrying dope in a van stolen from the same site as the JCB used in the Ballincalty raid. We linked them through a YouTube video someone conveniently made of the robbery. Rock junior told the Gardaí he and your father did the ATM job and they dismantled and dumped the vehicles in a bog swamp at a derelict site known as The Castle, that house once owned by your grandparents. In return, the son got only a suspended sentence and your dad got the bullet. But we're fairly sure the old man himself did the job with your dad and gave the son this info to keep him out of jail.'

I stared out across the resource area roof, over the tennis courts, down to the smoking wood.

'I think you know most of that and you found it out fairly recently. Maybe from Mr Rock who landed in Cloonloch the day your father got a release date. Didn't Rock get his share of the money? Or does he just want your dad's now as well?'

'How do I know?'

'Rock told you to get it for him, didn't he? That's why you shot at him.'

'Don't know what you're on about.'

'Someone claiming to be a resident tipped off the Gardaí Saturday night, shortly after the incident. He said Mr Rock had a supply level of cannabis in his boot. The resident named in the call later firmly denied ringing the Gardaí. But we did find the drugs in Rock's car. Who'd make a call like that?'

'No idea.'

'Someone who don't like Mr Rock too much, I'd say. You knew the drugs were found?'

'Ann told me, yeah.'

'Right. Did you know that as a result of the find in Rock's boot we were able to get a warrant on some of his registered properties up the country? We made some interesting discoveries. Stolen high-end motors and such. He's in a lot of bother because of that tip-off. And he is not very happy about it.'

'No?'

'Let's stop the messing, Tommy. You found out about Rock and his son screwing your dad. And then he arrives demanding your dad's share, or maybe the whole lot, for all we know. You planted the drugs to get rid of him, planning to tip us off later. Then you must have got pissed and decided you'd have a shot at him before he got locked up.'

'Where did you dump the taxi?' O'Keefe said suddenly, sitting up.

'I need the toilet.'

I sent a text as soon as I got out of the office. I took twenty minutes to walk across to the Resource Area toilets, wash my face, stalling a while at the front entrance, looking down the avenue. Back in the office, Armstrong was leafing through the school disciplinary manual. O'Keefe stared out the window.

I was sweating as I sat, not exercise sweat, this was an exam, waiting-for-the-dentist, asking-Rebecca-if-she-wanted-to-go-for-an-ice-cream-when-we-were-in-first-year type of sweat.

'What car did you say brought you home from Ballincalty?' Armstrong said, tossing away the manual.

'I told ye already, it was a red…'. I paused. I'd said something out of place. But I wasn't sure what, my mind blanked. I was tired. I couldn't do much more. They had the truth, the right story was on their side. I was lying and all they had to do was catch me out once.

I felt like just telling them what they wanted, to get them to leave me alone. I knew they wouldn't leave me alone though. They'd handcuff me there in the office, march me into their unmarked car. I'd be back in Trimon before night with the pool room lads who didn't like me anymore, or maybe someplace even worse.

'A red what?' O'Keefe said.

There was a knock at the door. Armstrong opened it. Johnny Marley entered, his tie hanging out over his laptop case.

'Detectives, sorry to interrupt. This young man is my client.' O'Keefe was already standing.

'We're just asking Tommy a few simple questions,' Armstrong said.

'What can I say, lads, it looks like a non-con interview to me.'

'Can I have a word outside, Johnny?' Armstrong said. They all went out into the hall. I couldn't make out what was said. There were footsteps, Johnny Marley came back.

'Good man, Tommy, you are keeping everyone busy.'

'I just texted Jake. I didn't know what all that was about. I can pay you at the mobile.' Talking to Johnny Marley then, with the detectives gone, it felt like a long cool drink of ice water on a hot summer's day.

'Don't worry about that. Come on, I'll bring you home. Your uncle was released without charge this morning. He wants a word with you urgently.'

We drove out to The Mackon in Johnny Marley's BMW. It had a massive digital dash. It reminded me of dad's new car, the one he got the week I started secondary school, the one he was in when they arrested him, with its walnut veneer and cool hands-free video phone set up. We hardly spoke as there were lots of calls. I loved the high-flying words from the range of voices: 'Repeal', 'Probate', 'Judiciary', 'Tribunal', 'Case Officer'. They excited me. I was jealous of Jake's new career. Every so often Johnny Marley would scroll through his iPad, finger files in the laptop bag between us. He smoked Majors constantly, beads of sweat broke out on his forehead. I sent a 'Cheers' to Marley. He texted back straight away: 'Let's go out. There's a new gimmick in Cloonloch, "Escape Hatch". I hear it's jammed the weekends, maybe this Thursday night?' It would be our first night out together since I'd been released.

The jeep was parked at the mobile. Inside, Ann sat on the far sofa bed, folding my clothes. Midnight was down at the end beside the toilet, hands in pockets, wearing his usual face of pain.

'Hello all,' Johnny Marley said.

'Thanks Johnny,' my uncle said.

'Not a bother. They're just probing. Tommy's an obvious choice given his record. They were hoping to squeeze him, get him on the hop when he was at school. One of their cheap tricks. But clever lad, he was able to text my P.A. and we got it sorted out. There's no evidence he had anything to do with the incident.'

The first thing I needed to do was write down the details of the green Vectra and the red Corolla and their imaginary drivers. But as soon as the solicitor's BMW was out of sight, Midnight grabbed me by the shoulder.

'Two nights I was stuck in that barracks!'

'It wasn't my fault you were there!'

'Think you're funny, do ya? Why did you break my window, huh? Council won't pay for that! Wind comin' in has me frozen!'

'Jeremy, calm down.' Ann was standing.

'Get off me!' I swung Midnight's big arse around, it rammed into the draining board. A plate fell off and smashed.

'Tommy!' Ann came between us. Midnight slipped as he tried to attack me, he fell backwards, ended sitting on the floor at the end of dad's bed.

'You young thug!'

'I didn't do anything!'

'Pock saw ya, plain as day! Now, where's the key for the rifle press?'

'Stop all this, or I'll call the guards myself!' Ann said.

Midnight tried to get up, pulling dad's blankets for support, a lot of mam's books slid on to the floor. Midnight grabbed the mattress, levered himself. He sat on the bed, pulled out the familiar yellow box. 'Young lads.'

He opened the plastic cover, bit the top of the cigar. 'I'll tell ya one thing, you haven't got a clue what you're dealing with there.'

'What the hell is that? Spoof talk?' My hands shook. I was really fed up of Midnight now.

'Come on, sit over here, Tommy.' Ann was at the far sofa. 'Calm yourself down.'

'Aisy for you woman. You weren't in my kitchen when them bullets started raining. If I—'

'Arra, shut up!' Ann said, 'You'd think you'd be used to that, being in all them great battles out in the Far East. The way you're talking, anyone'd think you spent the whole time in the spud house!' Midnight stared at Ann, his mouth open. 'Come on Tommy.' Ann led me to the table. 'I'll make us a cup of tea.' Ann poured water from the plastic drum into the pot, lit the gas. Midnight puffed slowly on his cigar. There was something soothing about the crackling noise of heating water.

'Ha!' Midnight said. 'Cups of *tae* will be no good to any of us if that bastard gets bailed out.' Ann brought over cups of tea to the table.

'We need to get that money, Tommy.' Midnight stared out the Perspex, through thick smoke. 'It's the only thing that'll quieten him. He'll never let this pass, you unloading a mag. on his window. He can't afford to. Everyone will be watching up in the smoke. He has to get satisfaction.'

'You're not listening to me as usual, Midnight. I don't know where dad put the money, alright?'

Midnight stubbed the cigar out on the carpet. 'I'm going down to the cottage to check in again between the stones in the walls. Say a prayer that I'll find it.'

Ann watched him walk awkwardly around the site and down the field.

'Cops checked all that already. They were here for days,' I said.

Ann started to pack the folded clothes into the sports bag.

'Am I going on holidays?'

Ann slid a bankcard across the table. 'The pin is 1976. There's about 1800 in it. Thumb it now to town. I'll say you went for a walk to clear your head.'

'What?

'I seen that Paddy Rock in the barracks. He was gone mad. I wouldn't like anything to happen to you, Tommy.'

'But he's inside now?'

'He has a lot of friends. Better go away for a few days, at least until your father is back.'

The shaver buzzed upstairs. I sat at the granite island in Marley's kitchen. I clicked down through the documents folder on his laptop. I found the PDF of medieval history. 'Got it online when I was doing the Junior. You read that, you won't need to go to any history class all year. Guaranteed,' Marley had advised. I emailed it to myself. I hovered over the videos folder, thinking I might find some dirty stuff, but when I clicked it, there were just a few pirated episodes of the zombie show dad used to love. I'd been watching it nightly since I got back to The Mackon, but Marley reckoned he'd gotten sick of it after the first season.

There was another root folder within, called 'Home'. Inside, I found hundreds of tiny AVI clips, mostly only a few megabytes. I knew they were things he used to post on Facebook, he didn't do that anymore. Scenes of someone throwing up at the Hallowe'en disco, or a couple shifting and pawing on top of a wheelie bin, that kind of slaggin' shite. Just as I was about to X off, I saw a clip that was last modified 3-9-13. Hard to forget that date, it was the night of the Ballincalty ATM raid.

I opened it up in VLC, clicking the mute. Marley was still shaving, but he'd not be long, for all the beard he had. O'Malley's forecourt came on the screen. The quality was much higher pre-YouTube pixel crushing.

Dad drove the JCB down off the flatbed. I watched the bucket scoop out the unit. I paused the video, zoomed in around the blob of Midnight, you could just see the numbers on the door of the truck.

Those numbers had linked Pock's son with the ATM raid. Marley had recorded the robbery from his bedroom window and put it up on YouTube. It was because of this video dad was in jail.

The shaver had stopped. I clicked off, erased the VLC viewing history as Marley came down the stairs, spraying deodorant. 'Taxi is on its way. Did you get it?'

'What?'

'The PDF?'

'Oh, yeah, yeah.'

'You alright? You look like you just seen a ghost?' I stared blankly at him. 'Tommy?'

The front door opened. It was Johnny Marley.

'Gentlemen,' he said, coming into the kitchen, carrying a newspaper. 'Are we going out on a school night?'

'Friday's a quiet morning, dad. I can study here till eleven.'

'Yeah, I'll believe it when I see it.' Johnny Marley opened a press, took out a foil-wrapped package of Italian coffee. 'You're a legal adult now, what can I do about it?'

'Not a thing!' They both laughed.

'So what's on tonight?'

'New thing in Cloonloch, "Escape Hatch".'

'What's that?' Johnny Marley squinted as he set up the percolator.

'It's like a warehouse with all these special rooms, you have to find your way out in a certain length of time.'

'So it's a maze?'

'Yeah, but there's more to it than that. Reviews are high-end.'

'Ye won't be late, will ya?'

'Nah.'

'Are you alright for money, Jonathan?'

I made a poor effort at hiding a laugh. It was the only time I ever heard Marley called that.

We got to the complex a bit early. There was a small pub next door. Marley decided we'd have a quick one. He was like a kid going to the circus. He scanned the website on his phone as we sat at the counter.

'You know it's actually got five different levels and this crazy final challenge!'

'We pick up Beck on the way home?' I said.

'She not coming to town?'

'Texted her earlier. Couldn't get away. Mother is laying down the law. She told me to call her when we're going home, she might sneak out.'

'Could be your lucky night, Tommy the boy.'

'Piss off.'

We had a fag at the door. It was like breathing again to get away from the conversation at the counter. Nothing Marley said anymore made sense to me.

Across the street, I saw a hooded figure hanging around one of the boarded-up units. In his baggy trackies, tucked in white sports socks, cheap cloth shoes and aimless circling the footpath as he scanned his phone, he was as near as any self-respecting drug dealer got to a shop window.

'There's a fella across there I know. Back in a minute.'

'Make it snappy, we're booked in at half seven.'

Billy smiled as I came across. 'Story, bud?'

'You know Liam from Trimon?' His smile faded.

'Who?'

'I'm O'Toole.'

'You what?'

'I was with Liam and them in Trimon until last May.'

'You the fella put that prick Masterson in the hospital?'

'Yeah.'

'So what do yiz want?' It was gone cold outside. I shivered.

'I was here all summer. They said I'd have two years out of this until you came back.'

'Yiz're done.'

Two lads from Junior Cert stopped. There was a quick exchange, they'd been my customers the week before. The whole thing would be on street cams, the guy was an awful dickhead.

'Do yiz want to fuck off?' the dealer said when the lads had gone.

'If it wasn't for me the last while, lads like them would have gone somewhere else. You'd have no trade. I want a split.'

'Don't bullshit me. There's always trade, bud.' Billy walked up the street to the town square.

I couldn't see anything, Marley was ahead of me in the darkness. They turned the lights on and off every few minutes, some weak attempt at suspense which didn't work at all, the glare lit up walls constructed from cheap MDF panels, painted with cell doors and bogus warning signs. They played silly noises in the background, as if you would ever hear chains rattling and chainsaws in real prison.

Even when the lights were off it wasn't completely black, there was a green glow from the exit doors which kind of ruined the whole illusion. You had to get through each 'chamber', all of them had a prison theme and a puzzle. You had to complete the course in less than sixty minutes. Soon after we started, it looked like we'd be out in fifteen. It wasn't much for a tenner each. We passed through the 'Interview Room', the 'Holding Cell' and the 'High-Risk Unit' without much trouble, the final section was the 'Parole Board'. It was a bit of an anti-climax, with its posters of bookshelves and boardroom style imitation walnut desk, all tacked on more sprayed MDF.

A final test had been set up at the centre with large wooden poles. The challenge was a version of an old matchstick trick I'd seen Midnight do hundreds of times when he was pissed on Dutch Gold in the mobile. He kept forgetting he'd shown it to me and I never bothered stopping him. Marley hadn't seen it before and couldn't solve it. I had to do it for him in the end.

He was almost frothing at the mouth when we got out. 'Savage craic, the real deal!'

We'd 'escaped' in less than twenty minutes. I thought we should ask for our money back, but Marley wouldn't hear of it, he was already typing on his phone. 'I'm gonna put a gold level review on this cat straight away! Great spot!'

We went into Lou's. It was a kind of retro place, 90s themed, football jerseys from the decade were tacked to the dark walls, an electric poker table hummed in the corner, the *Titanic* soundtrack played low on a loop. Thirtysomething couples sat at round tables near the windows, most of them looking in opposite directions or playing on their smartphones. Their drinks were at the same stage down the glass for ages, beer froth sticking dry to the sides. Marley took a large gulp of his pint. 'Ol' man out tomorrow?'

'Eight bells.'

'Rough what happened your dad, Tommy. Same for you though stuck in that place. Could have been me, easy enough. I'd have looked around that yacht like you did, deffo. I'd have done that dick you were getting hassled with. You never found out who told the cops about the Merc. that time?'

'No.'

'You did well to hold off on Eric. You'd have probably been let go if you put him in the soup.'

'Wouldn't do that.'

'Wet Room Trained, hah? No squealing under pressure.'

'If I did put them on to him, I'd be looking over my shoulder the whole time.' A bit like I was now. Marley took another drink, stared out the window for a few moments.

'You know, I never got the scanner off the internet that time.'

'What?'

'Eric rang me. I don't know, it was sometime in April that year. He'd heard from some lads we'd form with the cars. They gave him my number. He offered to set us up.'

'Why did you say you bought the stuff?'

'I don't know. Hard man shite, I suppose. I mean it was some toy to come on, eh?'

'Top of the range alright.'

'And he guaranteed to take the cars off us.'

'I often wondered how you met Eric.'

'Now you know, scan.'

But this new information hadn't improved a coldness already growing in me towards Jake Marley. I thought again of the video in his laptop. I felt loose inside, like there was a nail somewhere I needed to hammer.

I sat on the toilet lid. Fans whirred above my head behind the ceiling panels. The door in the cubicle was polished, free of marker graffiti. There was a distant mumble of voices in the bar, the door opening, and closing, the spring of the hinge, footsteps, zip, long stream into the urinal, zip again, sprinkling of water, the hand dryer for three or four seconds, footsteps, the door opening, spring hinge, the door banging closed. You didn't get the conversations here like in Lavin's: 'That fella has enough to retire on', 'Where's Peader today?', 'I wasn't looking at you at all, calm down!'

I sent Rebecca a text: 'Probably get a taxi soon. Eleven outside?' Smiley face came through. I tried Margaret O'Dea, but there was no answer. I didn't bother leaving a message.

I sat for a while, holding my head in my knees. I wanted to stay there for ever, staring at the tiles.

When I got back to the bar, there was something happening. Everyone was looking outside. Lou's had big clear windows across the front, you could see right into the street. Two guards were leading Billy into the back seat of a squad car. Marley was commentating on the episode to one of the couples.

'Where'd you go Tommy, you're missing all the craic!' He took his phone out. 'I just realised that sham is one of the ol' man's clients.'

Near the squad car, another man, in a blue garda jacket with the hood up, was putting something into a plastic garda bag. The cop looked a bit like O'Keefe, but I couldn't be sure. The dealer stared out the window as he was driven away.

'See you later dad.' Marley clicked off. 'He won't be home till God knows. What say we hit the basement, Tommy? Everyone'll be hyper now that Dope Deal is offline.'

'I told Beck we'd call for her around eleven.'

'Keep it under control, man! Tell her you got delayed and chillax!'

The taxi stopped in Ballincalty outside Marley's at half two. Johnny Marley's BMW was missing from its usual spot, probably still outside Cloonloch Garda station.

'Now, my good man, bring these calves to The Mackon.' Marley got out. He handed the driver a fifty. The driver pulled a tenner from somewhere. 'No, keep the change, scan. Tommy? Get to the Tate, that's all I can tell you. Get to the Tate.'

'Shut up you fool, you don't even know what the Tate is.'

'Listen, Tommy, I know as much about the Tate as your uncle knows about the Tote. Now, what do you think about that?'

'I think "Goodbye", and put a pint glass of water by the bed. And probably a bucket.'

'Ah, Tommy, you're some man. Some man, Tommy the boy!'

When we drove off, leaving Marley to collide with his garden wall, I turned to Rebecca. She smelt real good. I tried to shift her but she pushed me back. 'Calm down.'

'You're stone cold, that's the problem. I think Midnight left a few cans of Dutchie after him yesterday.'

'Cup of tea will be fine.'

'Jesus, you're fucking gorgeous, do you know that?' She blocked my grope.

'Your dad coming home tomorrow?'

'Eight bells, ma'am.'

'And what's he going to say when he finds me there?'

191

'Arra, fuck him! Four years, a lot of things change, you know, sexy?' I tried to get my hands under her blouse in the darkness as the taxi sped along the road to the bog.

The smell of coffee woke me. Rebecca was putting two mugs on the table as I turned around. She was already in school uniform. 'Jeez, you came prepared?'

'You've hardly any food here, Tommy. Where's the cornflakes?'

'I don't bother with breakfast. Where the hell are my fags?'

'It's the most important meal of the day, you know.'

'You're worse than Ann.' I threw one of the pillows at her. I had a headache and my stomach turned a bit, but it wasn't the worst hangover I'd ever had. I sipped the coffee, it was good. I found my Majors under the table.

'How are we getting to school?' Rebecca said, as she sat across from me.

'School? I don't know about that idea. I'm a bit ropey. Let's go to bed for the day?'

'You've got your exhibition, remember.'

'True. Tuohy goes to town on Friday mornings.'

'I hate travelling with him. He stares at me the whole time, Tommy.'

'He stares at everyone. He's alright. What time is it now?'

Through the Perspex, I saw a squad car pull up. Dad got out the passenger side, carrying a little red bag and a blue folder. He shut the door a little too firmly and never looked back as the guard drove away. I watched him walking through the green and yellow weeds. I could hear his footsteps as he came closer, the folder swishing through the air.

When he got to the door, I saw his jaw was really white. I'd never seen him so cleanshaven. Even though his eyes darted, his body moved slow. I saw lines on his neck and forehead I'd never noticed before, the cuffs on the prison shirt hung down to his knuckles. He stood at the sink and opened his top collar button. He scanned his bed, then the half-built house and down the field. He put the bag on the draining board, I saw his fingers shake. He turned to us. 'Tommy the boy.'

Now I looked down at him, but instead of feeling tall, it was more like he had shrunk. For a moment, I thought he was going to hug me. Then he looked at Rebecca.

'You know Beck?'

'Course I do. How are you?' He took a single cigarette from his shirt pocket, lit it and put the folder on the table. 'Ye going to school?'

'In a few minutes.'

'Do you have the phone handy there, Tommy? I've to make a call straight away to the poxy social worker. I'm meant to let her know as soon as I've landed. It's one of the parole conditions.'

He took my phone and went outside.

'Let's go.' I stood up, tossing some schoolbooks and copies into Marley's sports bag.

'Don't you want to tell him about the exhibition?'

'Like he'd want to come to that! Sure he doesn't even have a car!'

'He could get a taxi. Maybe he'll be getting a car today?'

'Nah.'

Dad came back in, gave me the phone. 'So ye're heading off now, yeah?'

We took up our schoolbags. At the door, Rebecca turned to dad. 'Tommy's art class have a public exhibition on today in the school . Tommy's project is meant to be unreal.'

'It's just a painting,' I said.

'Painting, huh? Bit of a Leonardo, are ya? Don't tell me you want to be one of them starvin' artists out in Paris or wherever. Get the schoolin', that's the way to go, son.'

'Bit late for that, dad. I'm two years behind everyone else.'

'Don't matter. Lad like you'll catch up.'

'You do need to play to your strengths, though,' Rebecca said.

'My strengths are to keep me head out of blue light.' Dad opened the fridge. 'Don't tell me you have no sausages?'

'We better go. Might see you at that thing, dad. It's at four.'

'We'll see, Tommy. I have to get some stuff organised. Get a car and a few block layers out to price the house.'

'You're going at the house again?'

'She'll be roofed by Christmas. We'll be out of this poxy sardine can by Paddy's day. There's going to be big changes around here.'

We waited for twenty minutes at the end of Tuohy's boreen until he came out. We watched him awkwardly step through the hole in his hedge and limp toward his jeep.

A taxi passed us, it pulled up at the mobile. A tall woman got out of the passenger's seat. She had long blonde hair, a yellow mini-skirt, white leather boots. It definitely wasn't Margaret O'Dea. My social worker had called me back a few times, but I hadn't bothered answering.

The taxi-driver killed the engine and took up a newspaper as the woman knocked and entered the mobile.

We started setting up for the exhibition around half three in the Assembly Hall. Marley had skipped his last class and gave me a hand carrying up the panel.

'Mad for the birds, scan,' he said, examining it, as we adjusted its position. The twenty-one birds were on the avenue, their beaks aimed at the scattered crusts. 'An artist from The Mackon, who would have seen it?'

Mr Coyne had arranged a zigzag walkway through tables of the A3 pieces, with my painting at the very end. I stood beside it, hands together, watching parents come and admire their children's work.

A few minutes later, I thought I was seeing things at the door. Margaret O'Dea was talking to Mr Coyne outside as she smoked a cigarette. He pointed down toward me.

'Tommy, you really are an artist!' she said, as she walked through the tables. 'Mr Sherlock mentioned the exhibition the last call I had with him. This is great…'. She looked at the birds for a few moments. Then she turned to me. 'I saw you tried to get in contact. Is everything alright? There was no answer when I rang back?'

'Sorry, that was a mistake. I pressed the wrong button.'

'You sure? I am glad I left work early to see this. Well done!'

'Thanks. I see you're back on the cigarettes?'

Margaret O'Dea's face coloured a bit. 'I'm afraid so. It's a stressful job, looking after artists like yourself, Tommy!'

We were just starting to tidy up at five o'clock when Midnight and Ann arrived. It was bizarre to see them in the Assembly Hall. They were so out of place, my uncle squinting at each piece as though they were hurting his eyes. Sherlock was at the door, glaring at Ann as she puffed on her e-fag.

'This is wonderful, Tommy,' Ann said, as they reached me.

Mr Coyne arrived beside them. 'Tommy's parents, is it?'

'Well—'

'Yes, Tommy is showing real talent in the Art Room. And I'm not just saying it. He's…', Mr Coyne lowered his voice and I could just hear him say to Ann, 'Quite frankly, he's in a different league.' Then he turned back to the painting. 'Now, what I like about this piece is the genuineness. It's art but it's also…', he looked up at the ceiling, like the answer was there, 'It's honest.' He pointed toward the first bird I'd painted, a little away from the rest. 'I particularly like this lone one out here. This sets off the entire piece, in my opinion.'

Midnight blew his nose with a scrunched-up ball of toilet paper. 'Yeah, yeah, now I'm no artist, but could you not have made some of them a different colour?' he said. 'A red or a green here and there.' He ran his hands through his curls, scattering dandruff on a table of blank sheets. 'Why do they all have to be black?

We went for some drinks to celebrate the exhibition in The Olde Tree. There was a lot of horseracing on the TV and it took some work to get Midnight to leave, but he wasn't the only problem. Me and Ann had to link Rebecca into the back of the Micra.

'We can't bring her home in that state,' Ann said. 'What was in that vodka? She only had a few.'

'She always gets like that. Can't seem to handle it at all.'

'Bring her back to the mobile for an hour. It's only nine o'clock. Let her sober up a bit and we'll bring her home then. We can talk to your dad. How is he?'

'Haven't seen him since this morning.'

It had been drizzling on the way out and by the time we got to the village, the rain was heavy. Behind the mobile, I saw a huge spotlight had been set up. The door at the front was open.

'What the hell is Joe at?' Ann said as she parked.

'Fuck it! Fuck it!' Midnight shouted, looking at the Perspex.

'What's wrong with ya?'

Midnight tapped his jacket. 'I left me wallet in The Tree. We have to go back straight away and get it.'

'Is it not empty?'

'No, it is not! I collected eighty euros this evening on the 6.10 at Newbury.'

'First I heard of this big win. We can get oil for the tank so, thank God.'

'We'll get no oil if we don't go straight back and get it.'

'Can't you ring him and get him to put it behind the counter?'

'Yeah, I know what he'll put behind the counter and what he'll put in his pocket. All you'll get back is the empty wallet, he'll say that's how he found it.'

'He's a businessman. He wouldn't do that, Jeremy.'

'They would all do that. Let's go woman!'

'What about Rebecca?'

'She can stay, it'll be alright,' I said.

I got out, opened the back door of the Micra, swinging Rebecca's lifeless arm around me.

'Give her a cup of coffee or something,' Ann said. 'It was a good day, Tommy. We were very proud in that school.'

'Let's go, woman!' Midnight's hands were shaking.

We collapsed onto the sofa bed. One of the bottles of Hennessey was open on the table. Zombies groaned as they chased people through a wood on the laptop. The spotlight out the back glared in through the Perspex.

Dad stared at me from the far sofa bed. He was sitting upright. His hands were on his lap like he was ready for take-off. He still wore the prison clothes, although they were now covered in clay.

I straightened Rebecca on the sofa, pulled her shoes off, put the blanket over her. I took up the bottle of brandy. 'Some of this left?'

I got a mug off the draining board and half-filled it. I drank it off the head, feeling the bite down my throat. I felt like shouting or something. I took up dad's Majors, pulled a fag out, lit it. I didn't much care about anything anymore.

'You didn't get to the exhibition in the end?' I looked directly at him as I spoke. I saw now his eyes were glazed. It was like there was some kind of dull filter between those white, grey and black dots and the world. He didn't move, hadn't since I came in.

'Busy with your social worker, I suppose,' I said, smoke smoothly clouding out. 'Fine bit of gear. I'd say–'

Dad leapt across the table, knocking the fag out of my hand, he grabbed me by the shoulders, like the way Midnight had done the day he'd came with Pock, but dad was much fitter and stronger, he lifted me with power, like a wave in the sea, dragged me towards the door.

I shouted but I didn't know what I wanted to say. We were outside, in the pouring rain, it stuck to my shirt, we stumbled backwards around the mobile. He dragged me into the light, the big spot blinded me with its yellow glare. I saw a hole freshly dug, the spade stuck at the edge. I tripped, my face landed on the soggy earth.

I couldn't see anything, only hear dad behind me, hoarse, deeper than usual, 'Where is it, you little prick?'

'Where's wha…?' There was grass and muck in my mouth.

'Don't fuck me around,' dad pulled me up, smacked me on the mouth, blood spilled from my lip. I was dizzy, there was a fist to the ribs, another to the stomach, it sank in, the blows were solid, steely, connecting. I couldn't breathe. I thought to fight back, but something made me lifeless. I just rolled on the ground toward the side of the mobile.

On the sitting room windowsill, I saw the other bottle of Hennessy, half full. Dad took it up, swigged it.

'This is what I get.' He put his other hand on the spade. 'I spend four years rottin' in jail and when I get out, I find my own wank stain has stolen from me.'

Dad stood over me, his shape huge in the spotlight's foreground. 'A slimy cunt of a drug dealer. So that's how you got the start with them. Bought your stake with my cash. I never thought I had to worry about you taking it.'

I was kneeling, my legs sinking into the softened ground, the driving rain stung my eyes. I could have been crying and I wouldn't have known.

'Where is it?' He roared into my ear. The drum rattled like a mega disco beat. 'Get it for me, or I swear I will kill you.' Dad lifted the spade. I got up, he adjusted his angle. 'This is what I get for trying to put manners on you. You come out of that place worse than when you went in.'

He came towards me. 'Where is my money?' My mind cleared for a second. I dived for the site doorway.

I heard him shout behind. I tripped over a wet and hardened bag of cement, banged my shin, it was pure agony. I rolled around the back of a wall stump, footsteps passed, heavy breathing, the brandy swishing in the bottle. I ran out the doorway, by the spotlight, my shadow huge on the side panel of the mobile.

Inside, Rebecca was snoring heavily. I pulled the Defence Forces keyring out. I opened the press over the cooker. Dad was still in the new house. Rain hit the Perspex and rolled down to the thin moss around the frames.

I assembled the Remington, fingers steady, clicked on the mag. I pulled the bolt back, released the catch, driving a round up the breech. I went back out, my thoughts dying away.

Dad was at the spotlight, his back to me, a cigarette burning in one hand. He drank the rest of the brandy, flung the bottle against the wall, it smashed to pieces. He swung around.

I pointed the Remington at him. He laughed without humour.

'What, do you think you're on television? Put that away before you shoot someone.'

'You told the cops I was at The Marina?'

Dad looked at the barrel of the rifle as he dragged on the last of his fag and tossed it into the hole. I clicked the lever from 'S' to 'A'. It was so easy to do. 'Put it down, Tommy. You've a lot of drink on board.'

'So have you. How come?'

'Twenty years. Liver is well rested.' He sounded strange, like he had swallowed barbed wire and it was stuck to his voice box.

'I didn't take your rotten money.' I tightened my grip on the rifle.

'I know, I know.' His face had softened, the cheeks had inflated out around the jawline, the eyebrows had risen, the forehead creased. But the eyes were still fogged. 'I had to be sure. Lads like you don't scare easy.' Raindrops rolled down dad's neck.

'You know that Midnight and Pock were out here searching the place?'

'Pricks.' Dad's face hardened again, but the heat was gone out of our words, we had a common enemy. 'Him comin' here for years every night with his cans of cheap lager and his rotten cigars, listening to him talking shite about Lebanon and as soon as me back is turned he shafts me. I never want to see that bollocks again.'

I lowered the rifle. 'How'd you know I was at the Marina?'

'I got a tip-off.' He was casual now.

'From who?'

'Are we getting in out of this rain? Johnny Marley alright?'

'How did he know?'

'He saw a poxy text on the young fella's phone. It was for your own good.'

'Do you know what Trimon Halls is like?'

'I didn't know you were going to try and steal a twenty-million-euro yacht, did I? And what did you do to

203

that young Masters fella? They weren't going to cut you loose after that.'

From the mobile, I could hear agonised screams. The zombies had caught up with the humans.

I saw Ash's thin bones in a pile then, gleaming yellow in the rain, on top of the dirt, tossed there like rubbish.

Dad saw me looking. 'I hadn't much time. I had to put it somewhere safe. If I dug a hole anywhere else, them detectives would have got it. They were looking everywhere.'

'I remember, dad.'

Dad looked at me oddly. It was like there were two men standing before me and they swapped places every few seconds. I didn't know which one was there until he spoke.

'You took it, didn't ya? You saw I'd dug up the grave? Who else would notice them stones moved?' He nodded, a smirk coming on his lips. 'You did. I knew it.'

Dad took a step forward, put his hand on the spade. 'Fuckin' youth! Where is it? Tell me! No cunt is goin' to con me out of my money!'

I raised the barrel. 'Stay back.'

'Gimme that rifle! I'll kill ya, I swear! Where's my money!' Dad came forward, the spade in the air.

'You shot my dog!'

'The money!' He jumped toward me, the spade swinging. I tripped back, finger on the trigger, the Remington jerked as the magazine emptied into dad's chest. He tripped back with the impact, his mouth opened. He dropped the spade, fell into the hole.

I couldn't breathe. Something squeezed my shoulder, then shook it. My lips were caked with dry scum, nose blocked, eyes stuck together. I pulled my eyelid open.

Midnight stood over me. I was lying on the far sofa bed, facing the road. Rebecca snored gently under the blanket across from me. Ann was at the sink. She rinsed cups, clouds of steam rose around her. 'Y'alright, Tommy? You don't look so good.'

'Hungover.' I sat up, looked around for fags. As I lit the flavourless thing, I looked up at the press over the cooker. The door was closed. I felt the Defence Forces keyring in my pocket.

'Where's Joe?' Midnight had sat beside me.

'He went off early.'

'Where?'

'The garage, I think.'

'Kilroy looked shut when I was passing. What happened last night?'

'Nothing.'

'What was the idea of the light out the back?' Midnight looked straight at me.

'I don't know. You'll have to ask him.'

'Is that girl alright?' Ann said. She went across, leant over Rebecca. 'She's as white as a sheet. We better get her straight home, Jeremy.'

'Let's have that tea you were making first, woman, for the love of God.'

'Hello? Are you alright, love?' Ann nudged Rebecca's shoulder. Rebecca opened her eyes wide, like she was caught in headlights. She got up, went around Ann to the toilet.

'Ah, the youth.' Midnight searched in his pockets.

Hangover symptoms began to intensify. My head was throbbing, stomach churning, throat furry. I looked back out through the Perspex, the ground was freshly raked. Ash's grave stones were in a pile at the mossy block wall. Flashes came into my head, heavy rain, wet clay, the spade, the rifle.

'Did you get your wallet, Midnight?' Nothing would have happened as it had if my uncle hadn't chickened out when he saw the brandy on the table.

'He found it as soon as we got to town.'

'It was the funniest thing. It was in the lining of me jacket the whole time. Never happened before.'

'And even funnier, his eighty euro wasn't in there either.'

'For the love of God, I already told you all that! It was a slip to collect eighty euros but a course I forgot I had put the winnings on the 7 o'clock at Newmarket. It's an accumulator thing.'

'Didn't accumulate much, did it?'

'At five to two, you would think—'

206

'Please!' Ann rose her hand, she was back at the sink. 'I don't want to hear any more about it. Your house was so cold last night, I had to go home, that's all I know. What came over your dad to go drinking, Tommy?'

'Don't know.'

'Was he in a mood?'

There was a deep cough from the toilet, spitting, moaning. Ann looked back at the door. 'Oh, the poor girl. And so young too.' Ann brought over the cups of tea, put them on the table. She folded up the blanket, sat across from us. She turned on her e-fag. 'I hope Joe is alright.'

'If he's still at it, it's the ones that cross his path I'd be worried about.' Midnight snorted, pulled out a screwed-up ball of toilet paper, blew his nose.

'Was he that bad, though?' Ann said. 'He hasn't drank for a long time. It mightn't affect him the same way.'

'That's not how it works with his type. Do you not remember? It used be aright at first going out with him, after he met Sheila. He was doing well then at the cattle dealing. He'd been at it since he was fifteen. He'd be rotten with money now if he was still trading. It was just before I signed up to the army. But he wasn't even twenty and he started hitting the top shelf near closing time. Shelia'd be conking and he'd always get into a row with some fella. He'd go pure loopy on the spirits. I'd leave them to it. He started calling me "The Midnight Man", because I'd always go after 12. I'd never wait on for late hours with him…'.

'I thought you always said you got that name because you saved some fella's life on night patrol? Out in Lebanon?' I said.

Midnight glared at me. Rebecca came out of the toilet.

'Sit down here love.' Ann waved Rebecca over. 'Take this cup of tea, it'll freshen you up.'

Rebecca shook her head slowly and sat on the sofa bed.

'We'll give you a lift home in a minute.'

Midnight tapped his cigar. 'Yeah, after he got that six months inside for nearly killing the fella with the shovel, he'd only ever take a can of coke after. It's a pity poor old Shelia couldn't do the same.'

There was a noise outside. A lorry had stopped. A man in a t-shirt and jeans covered in rust jumped out, hurried across the grass.

'O'Toole's?' he said, as I opened the door. 'Load for ye. Where do you want it?'

'Load of what? The man himself is not here.'

'Sand, fella!'

'Sand? Where does it usually go?'

'At the front of the site,' Midnight shouted. 'For block layers. He must have ordered it yesterday as soon as he landed.'

'That'll do.' The man nodded and went back to the lorry.

'He must be going building again,' Ann said, as I sat down.

'Reckons it'll be roofed by Christmas,' I said, before realising the reality.

'There'll be no roof on it, if that man is on the batter,' Midnight said, getting up. 'Come on, woman, I need to get back to Cloonloch before twelve.'

Rebecca followed them to the Micra. I hadn't space in my head to worry why she'd hardly spoken to me. I watched the driver edge the lorry in around the back. He pulled the short bars at the end of the truck. Then he operated the hydraulic lift with levers behind the cab. The back of the load was offered up to the sky. The fine brown sand tumbled out underneath the swinging steel back panel, on to the raked clay and covering Ash's grave stones

The detectives sat across from me, facing the site. Armstrong sipped his black tea. I'd fallen asleep again after Midnight and Ann had left, lain back on the sofa bed. I wouldn't have answered except I opened my eyes to find O'Keefe staring in through the Perspex.

'Having a lazy day, Tommy?' Armstrong said, as he opened his folder.

'Sort of.'

'Sorry to interrupt, but the Super sent us out. We got a report last night of a burst of gun fire around quarter to ten somewhere in The Mackon. The squad took a spin out, there was nothing amiss, but we're just checking with a few locals as well. You here all night yesterday?'

'From about nine.'

'You hear anything?'

'Nah. Watching that.' I nodded at the laptop. Zombies stumbled through a forest.

Armstrong smiled. 'That season 4? Turn it off, I haven't gotten around to that one yet. What about dad, was he here? Is he gone out this morning?'

I closed up the laptop. 'Gone to Kilroy's garage. Yeah, he was here last night.'

'Must be good to have him back. Did he hear anything?'

'Doubt it. He was in bed.' My mind cleared. 'Maybe it was Tuohy's crow repellent someone heard. He's a farmer next door. It goes off every so often. Sounds just like a rifle shot. It keeps birds off his spuds.'

'Makes sense. Although that wouldn't be a burst, would it? That'd be a single shot, no?'

'Is that him down there?' O'Keefe said, looking beyond me. I turned. Tuohy was at the corner of the field, where the old gap had been. He hammered staples into the top of the chunky new posts he'd installed. He was fitting a new line of barbed wire. 'I'll go out and ask him. He might run it for me.'

Armstrong wrote something down and closed the folder. I could hear O'Keefe's footsteps around the mobile on the gravel and weeds.

'Likely what it was. People are still high after the incident Saturday night. We already had a few bogus calls.'

I could hear faint voices down the field. It was mainly O'Keefe, with Tuohy probably only grunting responses.

'Paddy Rock is claiming he saw you driving the stolen taxi that night. And he thinks you planted the cannabis. Why would he say that?'

'I don't know, Detective.'

The voices in the field had died. Tuohy had started hammering again. O'Keefe's footsteps came back on the gravel. He went behind the mobile, near the load of sand. I thought I could hear his shoe crushing a steel casing. The Remington discharges empties through a trap in the breech.

But I was fairly sure the sand had covered them all. 'Maybe Rock is hot because he's inside now and dad's out with all that ATM cash? Couple of hundred grand never recovered. Not bad for four years inside?'

The mobile looked a lot different from the far sofa bed. There were no kitchen units on the other side, just the front door, the rectangular outlines of the toilet and shower unit, the Perspex facing the road. 'If he has it, I wish he'd start spending some of it.'

Armstrong laughed. 'Maybe that sand is the start.'

O'Keefe was at the door. 'Let's go.'

'Thanks for the tea, Tommy. You'll be here tomorrow, if we need to ask you any more questions?'

'Sure.'

I clicked on the laptop as they drove off. Something ground under my feet. I looked down. The carpet was caked with dried-in clay.

The nurse unplugged the drip feed from mam's arm, which now wasn't much more than a bone with loose skin. They'd put mam in a single unit. The room felt empty. I missed Nora pulling at my arm, thinking I was Gerald come to collect her, or the woman that always slept across from us, eyes tightly shut, blankets tucked around her chin.

'Just taking this out for a second, Shelia,' the nurse said, but mam's eyes were tightly shut.

Midnight burst into a bout of coughing, a desperate attempt to drive up the phlegm in his throat.

'Will you go outside and do that, spreading germs in the hospital!' Ann said.

'It's the pipes, woman, I have to clear me pipes!'

The nurse plugged back in the drip.

'When do you think she'll be able to go back to St Michael's, nurse?' Ann said.

'That's up to Dr Karl. Hypoglycaemia has developed as a result of the Wernicke's.'

'What's that?'

'The consultant will assess her again on Monday, Miss Gillhooley.'

'An awful sight,' Midnight said. 'When we were all going out years ago, never thought it'd end up like this. Ah! I'm going out for a smoke.'

I watched my uncle waddle to the corridor. Ann looked at me. 'Did you say you were meeting Rebecca this evening?'

'Yeah. Ye can drop me at the hotel after.'

'You never took out that money?'

'Nah. I have the card here–'

'Keep it for now, love. I'm worried about your father, if he's drinking. You might change your mind in the next few days. And don't forget to bring your schoolbag with you. It's still in my car.'

'Ah, I'll leave it there till Monday.'

'Bring it with you. You might do a bit of study tomorrow.'

Ann opened her handbag and took out a passport. 'I applied for this a few weeks ago. I thought you might need it.'

'That an old photo?'

'I got it off the Principal, and the Garda in my village is very obliging, he stamped it for me.'

'Thanks.' I looked at the photo. It had been taken when I was in first year.

'You haven't really changed that much at all,' Ann said, as she closed her handbag.

I stood at the edge of the function room dancefloor. Music boomed from a three-piece on the stage to my right. Lads in suits danced in front of me, collars turned up, ties loosened, bouncing in one messy group, arms over shoulders. I could hear the drunken words 'We are the lads, lads, lads, we are the lads, lads, lads, hi-hu!'

Amongst them, the bride emerged laughing, a bottle of Britvic 55 in her hand. She hugged every second person she met. As she came off the floor, she caught my eye. 'Well you! I asked Donal and he doesn't know you or your friend!'

'I suppose you got me. But I'm adding to the atmos.!'

'I'm sure you are! Gatecrash a lot of weddings, do you?'

'We didn't make it downstairs to the disco, to be honest.' I nodded at Rebecca, her head was flat on the tablecloth.

'What's wrong with her?'

'Vodka. Knocks her out every time.'

'God love ya.'

'Good luck with everything.'

'You're very sweet!' Someone took her hand and she was gone.

My phone vibrated. Text. 'Outside now.'

I took the sports bag from under the table, slid the cash into an inner compartment and walked around the dancers. Another group had joined the men, heavily make-upped women of thirties or forties, they wore flowery dresses, they were head-banging and playing air guitar.

I went through the double doors, down carpeted stairs. The glass exit doors were open. At the far end of the carpark, an ambulance was parked up on the kerb, the driver's door open, indicator flashing. I stopped and looked around the lobby. There was a noise behind me. I turned, the keyring across my fist.

It was someone from the wedding, tie loose, red-faced. He dribbled as he came to the end of the stairs.

'Ya lost, scan?' He laughed, pushed past me.

The toilet door slammed. I heard roars, the hand-dryer crashed and whirred. I ran out the double doors, I could hear Pock shouting through the window. I dropped the keyring by the ambulance.

There were only a few passengers on the night bus. I sat halfway down. I took out my phone. The number rang for ages. 'Yes?'

'Is this Mann's?'

'Yes?'

'Your daughter, Rebecca—'

'Oh my God, is she alright, oh no—'

'She's fine. She just needs to be collected from the function room of the Cloonloch Arms.'

'Is that you, Tommy?'

I hung up. The digital clock over the driver changed to 00:00. He started the engine. We moved through the streets. Lads tripped over each other on the way to the late bars and clubs. I saw flashes of short skirts, loose shirts, a fella trying to get the ride in an alley, jeans at his ankles. Chip bags, burger wrappers and snack boxes were scattered around the paths. At an open vent somewhere, I could hear bursts of shouting, laughter. Through the glass, it looked like a mad scene in a movie.

A Gardai squad car passed us, the spinning light flashed into the bus for a second. I thought of dad in the mobile, keeping his head out of the blue rays, what Rebecca had said about playing to my strengths.

I checked everything in the sports bag. There was a short pencil rolling around at the bottom beside a crumpled green copybook. I took them out, flicked open the copy. It was multi-purpose, I'd used it for every subject since I came back from Trimon Halls. There were scribbled maths formulas, geography sketches of the Earth's layers, a piece of writing about some war. It had started life as my first-year English writing copy. I turned to the front. After I'd written a description of myself, there was a short composition about what happened to Ash. The handwriting seemed so young, big boxy letters, curls everywhere, circled dots.

The story had gotten a 'B+' and a comment 'Demonstrates a talent with words. Keep it up!' I sat back, watched the last of the streets go by, then the industrial estates, with huge yards and rows of trucks, then houses, big gardens lit up, then small windows of cottages, a yellow beam across a hay shed, a tractor beside a turf stack. The last of the town glow faded into the country dark. I clicked on the overhead light and turned over the page.

The Mackon Country is Martin Keaveney's second novel. His debut novel *Delia Meade* was published in 2020 and followed a short story collection, *The Rainy Day* in 2018, both published by Penniless Press. Stage and screen credits include Ireland's national broadcaster RTE and Scripts Ireland Playwriting Festival. He has a PhD in Creative Writing and Textual Studies. Scholarship has been published widely, including at the *New Hibernia Review, Journal of Franco-Irish Studies* and *Estudios Irlandeses*. He was awarded the Sparanacht Ui Eithir for his research in 2016. He works as a creative writing lecturer/consultant (see more at *www.martinkeaveney.com*).

DELIA MEADE

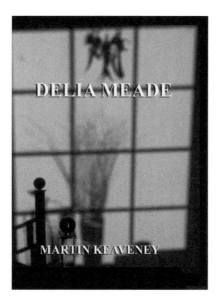

Now the last of Delia Meade's children have married and moved away, she decides to tidy up the little room under the stairs, known as the Glory-hole. Amongst the forgotten toys, worn-out clothes and dusty boxes of photographs, Delia travels through happy and sad decades of her time at 109, Bog Road. *Delia Meade* was published by Penniless Press in 2020.

'An excellent debut.'

Connaught Telegraph

Purchase *Delia Meade* at www.mayobooks.ie and many other outlets.

THE RAINY DAY

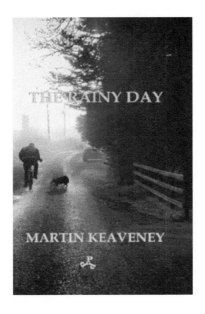

Farmers: young and old, cunning, foolish, greedy, generous, talented and forgotten. These and those belonging to them are gathered in this short story collection, sometimes clearly in Ireland's west, but mostly in an unnamed landscape which shapes those often waiting for that rainy day to come. *The Rainy Day* was published by Penniless Press in 2019.

'*The Rainy Day* […] will really strike a chord with rural readers.'

Connaught Telegraph

Purchase *The Rainy Day* at www.mayobooks.ie and many other outlets.